Homecoming

A Sci-Fi Novel

BY ELIZABETH CHANG

ISBN: 978-1-09830-495-9 (print)
ISBN: 978-1-09830-496-6 (ebook)

Dedication:
For my father who is always in my heart. And for my children
– you are my everything.

Thanks to:
Susan Burroughs, Ted Schipper, Randy and Ruthie Greenberg,
Elisabeth Barek, and special thanks to my Mother, Step Father and
Husband for your love and support.

Table of Contents

FOREWORD

"The future is already here, it's just not evenly distributed."

~ William Gibson

Humanity is us, but we are not the same. We hope that we are evolving towards a better version of ourselves. However, that evolution is not a strait trajectory and progress is not evenly distributed.

Elizabeth Chang crafts an exciting interplanetary adventure where space is capricious and unpredictable. This story is a grand adventure on an epic scale where familiarity and strangeness are woven together with seamless ease. Her ideas about science are revolutionary, and her sense of adventure is timeless.

Like many star ships of 20th century Sci-Fi, the cautious optimism of this novel offers inspirational models for science and culture. Yet, Chang stretches the possibilities with new ideas about the underlying principles and purpose of technological development.

Chang has resolved some of the major issues of our own time in elegant and captivating ways while other problems continue. She explores solutions to the problems caused by our manufacturing practices and material culture with intriguing ideas inspired by the latest research and a sincere love for the natural world. The technologies she creates also span interplanetary scales and explore the practical application of cutting-edge quantum theory.

Although humanity has come together to solve catastrophic problems like global climate change, regionalism and sexism persist. Though humanity has traveled beyond the solar system, major economic powers on Earth scheme against each other. Chang writes women who are brilliant, graceful, and loyal in the face of cultures that insist on their compliance and dependence.

~Susan Burroughs

CHAPTER I:
THE WEDDING

It was a beautiful garden wedding that nostalgically harkened back to bygone years: android waiters dressed in old-fashioned twentieth-century uniforms circulated with trays, serving amuse-bouche and ice-cold glasses of champagne, and golden rays of light illuminated silhouettes of the elegantly dressed guests as the sun slipped slowly behind the softly rolling Tuscan hills.

Deftly moving through the attendees like a dandelion seed floating on a summer breeze, Ella made her way to an ivy-covered wrought-iron gate displaying an assortment of decorative vintage brass keys. Attached to each key with a ribbon was each guest's name and table assignment.

Thumbing through the keys, Ella couldn't help but overhear the two ladies next to her gossiping. "Did you see the enormous bow on the back of her wedding gown?" one said.

"She looked like Minnie Mouse scurrying down the aisle!" remarked an impeccably dressed giraffe-like-lady, her stiletto heels sunk two inches deep in the muddy grass.

"And his face was beet-red! I heard he didn't even make it back last night…" Her prim friend half-whispered.

Ella pretended not to listen as she looked around for a familiar face. The groom, Dave, was a friend of her husband James.

Although Ella had hardly met the bride, Xing-Xing, she seemed nice enough and didn't deserve such prattle, especially on her special day. Ella could scarcely find a friend in the crowd amongst the sea of wedding guests.

Across the garden, she caught a glimpse of James' mischievous eyes as he engaged in a lively conversation with his old pals from university. His gaze caught hers, and for a split second, the suggestive half-curl of his lips made her blush. Time seemed to stand still.

The clanking sound of a knife against a glass caused all conversation to come to a halt. The father of the bride, Ker, raised his glass. "Thank you all for coming here today to help us celebrate the union of my daughter, Xing-Xing, to this most unworthy fellow…"

There were giggles and laughter all around. "Just kidding!" Ker said with a smile. He put an arm around Dave. "We couldn't have dreamed up a more deserving son-in-law. Dave, we are proud to welcome you into our family. And now everyone, please make your way to the veranda. Dinner is served!"

Ella followed the meandering tide of guests as they made their way through the garden and up a few stone steps to an outdoor sitting area. Long tables had been set up for dinner; opulent floral displays of white and green hydrangeas, roses, orchids, baby's breath, and freesia ran down the center of the tables and cascaded over the edges towards the grass.

Ella found her seat next to James at their pre-assigned table. He affectionately tucked a wisp of her auburn hair behind her ear. "Don't they look lovely?" Ella said as she admired the newlyweds.

James paused before answering. "I'm not sure I see a match," he finally said.

"Oh, really?" Ella raised an eyebrow.

"She's full-blown Asian Union, and he's West Coast American Union. What do they really have in common?" James said half-seriously.

"I don't know—maybe chemistry?" Ella smiled coyly as she sipped her glass of dark red wine.

Ella and James were coming up on their two-year wedding anniversary. They met during their third year at Oxford when Ella was 20 and James had just turned 21. Six years later they were married at Christchurch and had a small reception at Le Manoir Aux Quat'Saisons.

"Remember what it was like when we first met?" Ella said with a wink.

"Yes, I do," James said. He smiled back at her as he remembered how they couldn't keep their hands off each other, snogging in the backseats of borrowed cars and behind wooded patches of trees in the university gardens. They'd even shagged on the rooftop of the Senior College Room during a spring holiday.

It had been two years since the birth of their son, Max, and their initial passion and attraction had turned into steady love and admiration. They shared the kind of supportive mutual respect that could sustain a marriage through the best and worst of times. Ella felt that the more she got to know James, the better she understood him and more she loved him. And although James generally shied away from introspection, he knew that he couldn't live without Ella.

James recalled the first moment he had met Ella. It was the night of the Trinity Ball. He had heard all about this wonderful girl, the perfect girl, the girl who was smart, beautiful, kind, and patient… and he had heard all of that from his friend Michael, who was dating Ella at the time.

It was twilight, and the festivities were in full swing. A thousand bright-faced students swarmed the commons. Through the crowd, James could still remember seeing Michael and Ella approach him. Michael introduced Ella to James. When they shook hands, James felt a shock of electricity; somehow, he knew this was the girl he was supposed to marry. *This* was the woman he would spend the rest of his life with, the woman he would have a family with, the woman he would grow old with.

Then he had shaken off the thought, chalking it up to the exorbitant quantities of bubbly he had consumed. Still, James couldn't keep his eyes off Ella for the rest of the night. At one point, he saw the spaghetti strap of her midnight-blue dress accidentally fall off her shoulder. He tried to stifle an audible groan by patting his face with his napkin and pretending he had indigestion. Nevertheless, the wife of the dean of Christ Church indignantly shot him a dirty look as she passed by.

When James looked up again, Ella was putting the strap back in place. She continued walking until she was out of his sight. Somehow, even though she was dating his friend, James felt certain they would end up together.

The following afternoon, James and Ella had met up in the Bodleian Library to "study" together. Afterwards, they went for a walk through Port Meadow. A short conversation turned into a multi-hour heart-to-heart. Despite growing up on opposite sides of the planet—James in Ithaca, Greece, and Ella in Woodside, California—they felt like they had surprisingly similar symmetry in their lives, which they took to be a sign that they were meant to be together. For one thing, they both had pets named Echo: Ella's Echo was a small dog that a classmate had given to her after his family could no longer care for it, and James' Echo was a stray cat that he had taken in around the same time. They both had entrepreneurial, workaholic fathers, and they both had little sisters who had passed away in childhood. James had been six when his mother gave birth to a stillborn baby girl, he told her.

Ella's voice cracked a little when she tried to recount the story of her own sister. "It happened when I was babysitting… I had been annoyed that my parents made me look after my little sister, Rose…"

James could tell she was nervous. He rested his hand on hers reassuringly, and the warmth of his skin against hers somehow gave her courage to continue.

"While we were playing at a park, I was reading *The Hobbit*," she went on. "I didn't notice when Rose disappeared. When I looked up from the book and realized she was gone…"

She hesitated again; James squeezed her hand and waited patiently for her to continue. "I searched for her," she finally said. "I ran up and down the streets of Menlo Park, but I couldn't find her."

Ella's parents called the police and they put out an amber alert, she told James. For months, officials looked for Rose. Her parents reluctantly but eventually came around to the idea that something terrible must have happened to her. Had she been kidnapped? Abducted? The authorities insisted that Rose was almost certainly deceased.

Ella continued to wait and hope, posting about her missing sister on social media for two years. Three years later, after she had given up hope, Rose was found—she was being held hostage in the home of a forty-eight year-old man. Ella's parents brought her home, but Rose was so damaged and hurt and confused that she never completely recovered.

The pedophile was put in a correctional facility and was undergoing sexual perpetrator therapy and behavior modification genetic engineering. Rose had biweekly therapy sessions with an expert in the field, who tried to help her cope with her PTSD. She started taking pills to help her sleep and inadvertently became addicted. At one point, Ella's parents discovered that Rose was sneaking alcohol, and they threw away all of the alcohol in the house. But then, late one night, when everyone was asleep, Rose took too many pills and never woke up.

Ella had never forgiven herself or her parents for giving up on her sister. Had Rose been found earlier, Ella believed that her little sister would still be alive. Even today, many years later, she sometimes couldn't stop thinking about Rose and what her life might have been like.

"Ella, is everything okay?" Ella felt James' hand rubbing her arm, and she realized she had been staring off into space. Sometimes she found herself reliving painful memories and losing track of time.

With an effort, she pulled herself back to the present. "Oh, yes, it's a lovely wedding," she murmured. An android server placed a plate of ginger-soy sea bass and medium-rare-cooked prime rib in front of her. The bass and prime came from local labs in the EU—and were grown without a brain, of course. Organic old-vine Amarone was poured into crystal glasses.

Grateful for the distraction, Ella turned her attention to the holographic display that was replaying videos of the bride and groom's lives leading up to the wedding. Unflattering haircuts, geeky school portraits, ski trips, and lower-school graduations mixed together in a video montage that was set to nostalgic semi-cheesy music. Much better to chuckle at that than feel melancholy or mournful, she decided, and forcibly turned her thoughts away from Rose.

Dinner came to an end and the wedding attendees meandered back into the ancient stone villa. A gilded ballroom decorated with well-kept antiques glowed in the soft light of living lamps made of plants genetically modified with florescent jellyfish DNA and strategically positioned along the edges of the room. Purple-glowing ivy clung to the baseboards and set a romantic mood. Amongst the delicate setting, Xing-Xing and Dave were introduced for the first time as "husband and wife," and everyone applauded.

Ella and James had entered the ballroom together, but then they had drifted apart as each of them had curiously gone their own way to inspect the glowing plants. Now Ella looked across the room and saw Eleanor, James' high-school girlfriend, standing on one side of him. Linda, his first-year university girlfriend, was standing on his other side.

Eleanor had never completely forgiven James for forgetting to officially break up with her when he left for university. She learned of their split when she saw Linda posting pictures of the new happy couple on social media. For her part, Linda had never understood why James had called their relationship quits after just one term. (Truthfully, she swore too much for his taste, and besides, he had known almost immediately that she just wasn't "the one.") James had always been rather direct and hated to waste time and effort, so he felt he had been doing them both a favor by moving on. The three of them exchanged awkward glances.

James excused himself from the trio and headed across the room towards Ella. She couldn't help but find his situation rather amusing.

On a raised stage, a retro jazz band played "Fly Me to the Moon." Dave led Xing-Xing out into the center of the dance floor. He spun her around and pulled her in close, their bodies swaying in unison. The guests stood at the edges of the room, observing the first dance, gossiping and joking over the loud music.

On his way to Ella, James ran into some old pals from university. "Dave told me that she made him take dance lessons for six months," Michael said to James, chuckling.

"Poor bastard!" Andrew snorted, putting his arm around James' shoulder and taking a swig of his Pimm's Cup.

James had rowed with Michael and Andrew when they were at Oxford together. Ah, those were the good old days! Punting on the Isis, drinking Pembroke's private collection of wines at high table, and discussing politics and philosophy into the wee hours of the night. After graduation, Michael had returned to the Asian Union and Andrew had taken a city job that kept him flying around so much that he spent more time in the air than at any of his flats. He liked to keep at least one on every continent, fully stocked, and AI maintained with an android housekeeper, ready for any last-minute visit.

Xing-Xing's skin-tight sparkling gown of live, genetically designed fish scales hugged her petite figure and reflected the light of the glow lamps in a thousand shimmering prisms. The song came to an end, but without missing a beat, the band glided into playing "Witchcraft." Xing-Xing's father cut in "to show the young groom how it's really done," as he put it, and Dave walked over to take his mother's hand. A few other guests joined in; soon, the dance floor was packed.

Ella dragged James away from his friends and pulled him onto the dance floor, ignoring his hesitation. She loved to dance so much that she pretended to overlook her husband's shockingly poor sense of rhythm. Fortunately for all involved, however, the music promptly switched to a slow dance.

Ella stepped in close, and James put his arms around her waist. Swaying from side to side was almost impossible to mess up, even for him. In her heels, Ella was almost his height, and they could dance cheek-to-cheek. His short stubble tickled her; she could smell whisky on his breath.

Ella brushed away a dark curly tress that had fallen over his forehead and into his eyes. Sea-blue and delightfully mischievous, James' eyes were the feature Ella loved most about her husband. She was well aware that she had been a "catch" and could have had her choice of any of the young lads at school. While James was handsome, he wasn't the best-looking or the most athletic, but Ella had fallen in love with his intellect, persistence, and confidence.

Ella had had a couple of boyfriends before James. Mostly, they had gone to parties together, held hands, and awkwardly kissed a few times. It wasn't that she had wanted to "wait for marriage" to do more—that felt antiquated, as though her virginity were a commodity to keep locked away for some kind of medieval transaction—but she had wanted to wait for the first time to be with someone special, someone she truly loved.

After a couple months of dating, James had surprised Ella one weekend by flying them back to his family's home. Located close to the pristine beach of Agios Loannis, Ella had been enchanted by the traditional stone house and the stunning views across the Kefalonia Straight. They let themselves in just after sunset. "They've gone out to an event," James assured her. He lit an old-fashioned wood-burning fire and put on a hologram movie. That night, with his arms around her, looking into his deep eyes, she knew that she loved James more than she had ever imagined she could love anyone. Later, they made love for the first time in his childhood bedroom. Then they spent the weekend exploring his stomping grounds, playing board games, and sneaking back and forth between her guest room and his room late at night.

"Has anyone told you how beautiful you look tonight?" James whispered in Ella's ear. She wore a dark purple gown made of genetically modified silk that looked slightly iridescent. The soft fabric gathered in folds around her bust and twisted up into braids over one shoulder.

With a laugh, Ella dismissed her husband's compliment.

James found it rather charming that his gorgeous wife never accepted a compliment. He could never quite read her—she was a mystery wrapped in an enigma that was trapped in a black hole. And he wanted nothing more than to spend his life trying to decipher the riddle that was Ella. As the song paused, James and Ella made their way through the tall French doors to the outside.

The courtyard was set up with high tables decorated with floating tea candles. A cool breeze chilled the air as Androids offered complimentary pashminas to the ladies and freshly rolled cigars to the gentlemen. Guests stood around sipping tea and nibbling on finger cookies, miniature crème brûlées, and petite chocolate-raspberry mousse cakes sprinkled with gold leaf. Android servers passed around slices of layered strawberry-vanilla wedding cake.

It had been a long day. After politely nibbling on some of the cake, James and Ella headed over to the queue at the valet.

"James, old man, let's not let another three years pass before we get sloshed!" Michael came up from behind, slapping James on the back.

"First round's on you!" James replied with a grin.

Michael turned to admire Ella. "More lovely than ever…" He bent over to kiss her hand.

"Alright, stop putting the moves on my girl! You had your chance already," James joked.

The old friends chuckled and made their farewells as Michael stepped into his eagle vehicle and flew off into the starlit sky. A few seconds later, James' eagle vehicle landed steps away from the attendees. The android valet politely handed James his keys.

He and Ella stepped into the feathery upholstered interior. The vehicle was the body of a genetically engineered massive eagle with a computer in place of a brain. The feathers had been engineered for enhanced photosynthesis that generated enough energy to power the metabolism of the body and the battery of the computer.

James and Ella sat down. The doors shut and the seatbelts fastened themselves.

"What is your destination this evening, sir?" the computer asked in a standard British-European Union accent.

"Take us home," James replied.

Ella rested her head on his shoulder and closed her eyes. She'd had a little too much to drink, and her head was starting to spin. She felt the vehicle lift off and swoop through the air.

"Estimated travel time is 2 hours and 36 minutes," the computer stated.

Precisely 2 hours and 36 minutes later, they landed on a grassy patch outside of their home on the Greek island of Ithaca. James helped Ella out of the vehicle, and she leaned on his arm as they walked up the path to their home. Midway across the field, she took off her shoes and walked barefoot through the grass. The scent of wet earth and the lulling sounds of crickets soothed her senses. The spinning feeling from the wine and the flight gradually subsided.

The house was a large complex of intertwining aspen trees that had been grown together into the shapes of rooms, hallways, doors, and windows. The slim white trunks formed textured living walls; the branches reached towards the sky in a vaulted roof formation. At the roots of the trees grew a collection of colorful, genetically enhanced fungi. The system was symbiotic: the trees captured carbon from the atmosphere and transformed the carbon into sugars, and then fungi sucked the sugars out of the tree roots and decomposed the sugars, thereby restoring the carbon into the earth.

When James touched the door, the sensors in the handle recognized his DNA. The branches that formed the door parted down the center, allowing James and Ella to pass through before returning to their closed state.

"Welcome home!" Hestia, their android, greeted them at the door. She took their coats and hung them in a nearby closet.

"How did everything go with Max tonight?" Ella inquired.

"Splendid," Hestia replied. "At 5:42 pm, Max had pumpkin risotto and kale chips for dinner and then berries and ice cream for dessert. After that, we played with magnetic blocks and made a fort in the living room. I read him three stories before bedtime. He has been sleeping since 8:02 pm."

"Thank you," Ella said. She had deliberated for quite some time before choosing an android for their household, and when she did, she had chosen an android with housekeeping and nanny programing. So far, Ella had been pleasantly surprised—Hestia seemed to know what to do with very little instruction. She was great with Max and very helpful around the house. In fact, Ella could scarcely remember what she had done before Hestia. She had practically become part of the family.

Ella tiptoed down the hall. "Pallas, show me Max," she whispered.

A miniature hologram of Max's room appeared in the air, projected from a recess computer panel, and made Ella smile. There was nothing sweeter than the sight of her sleeping baby.

James was following close behind her. To the delicate ears of a mother, his footsteps sounded like stomping elephants. "Shhhhh!" Ella warned her husband. She checked again; thankfully, Max was still sleeping soundly.

"He's fast asleep," James said dismissively as he swiped the hologram away. He scooped Ella up in his arms and carried her to their bedroom.

In the center of their bedroom was a living bed, with posts made of four olive trees that had been grown together in a beautiful woven branch formation. The branches intertwined to support the mattress and create a canopy above.

Glow ivy clung to the walls, its soft light warming the room. "Skylight open," James said as he threw Ella on the bed. The vaulted branches above parted, revealing a starlit summer night.

Ella stared at the twinkling stars as James kissed the little hollow place just below her neck. She felt his body press into hers and closed her eyes. A wave of desire passed through her like the steady rhythm of the ocean's tides.

CHAPTER 2:

ELLA

Ella woke suddenly from her dream. Not just any dream—*the* dream. The dream she kept having over and over. And once again, just before she was about to make love to her husband who had been gone for so long, she woke up.

Glancing across the bed, she saw that his side was still made, his pillows untouched. The living bed he had made for them—the bed that had once brought her so much joy—felt empty, sad, and barren in his absence. She'd started to hate the bed. It had come to symbolize the perfect man, the man she had long ago put on a pedestal, the man who had disappeared and had been beyond her reach for twenty years. Ella wanted to throw the bed out, but it was literally growing out of the ground. And in a way, destroying the olive trees felt like it would be a physical assault on their marriage.

It had been nearly twenty years since James had left for Hectar and ten years since anyone had heard from him. She knew she should give up and move on. And part of her *wanted* to move on, but she couldn't shake the feeling that James was still out there. Part of her resolve traced back to what had happened to her little sister—had Ella looked a little harder for Rose, she might still be alive today, Ella thought. She had vowed never to make that same mistake again. As long as there was even a sliver of a hope that James was out there, she was going to keep looking. Deep down, she wondered if his disappearance was all her fault. "Careful what you wish for," her mother had always told her.

Although their marriage had looked perfect from the outside, Ella and James had had their share of problems. Deeply in love and highly sensitive, they tended to end up arguing about nothing. During one weekend getaway to London early in their relationship, she remembered, a stupid argument about traditional English and French gardens had ended with Ella storming off and James chasing after her. And things had only gotten worse after having Max. Who should get up with him in the middle of the night? How long should they breastfeed him? Ella and Max disagreed more than ever after the tiny human had entered the picture. At one point, a few months before James left for Hectar, Ella recalled secretly wishing James would go away and never return.

Now Ella was approaching 50, and a few grey hairs had started to blend into her wavy auburn hair. She lay in bed wishing she could take back her stupid wish from twenty years before.

It was hard to leave the comfort of the bed—she wanted to cling to the sleepy memory of being with James for as long as possible. However, the sun was up and work was calling. Today was an important day in the office, and she needed to be on time.

She closed her eyes, counted to three, and then forced herself out of bed. Dragging herself into the shower, she let the hot water run over her head and down the small of her back for a long time. Then she got dressed, carefully selecting her clothes and accessories to appear fresh, effortless, and powerful. *Men have it so easy,* she thought to herself. *They can wear the same thing every day and no one would notice.* On the other hand, women—even in this day and age—would be evaluated, scrutinized, and picked apart based on their appearance.

On her way out the door, she peeked at Max. In the holographic image of his room, she saw that he was still sleeping. Everything in the room looked just as it always did in the dream, only Max was now 22 years old. "Pallas, when Max wakes up, tell him I've gone into the office and ask him to meet me there for lunch," Ella said as she put a few items in her briefcase.

"Affirmative," replied the computer.

At the office, refreshments were being served in a conference room where the quarterly board meeting was about to be held. As the board members filed in, they helped themselves to the array of food and drinks: Robert, one of the older board members, who had been James' professor at Oxford, poured himself a double whisky, while Vince, who was one of James' oldest friends, helped himself to caviar-topped deviled eggs. He had just stuffed a particularly large egg into his mouth when Ella stepped into the room.

"Gentlemen," Ella said as she took her seat at the head of the table, "it's nice to see you're making yourselves at home."

Vince looked up momentarily and brushed some egg debris off his shirt.

Ella politely continued, "Let's call this meeting to order." She nodded at the secretary to begin taking minutes. "The first order of business is still our effort to find our crew who went missing after retrieving Project Stella. Unfortunately, our scouts returned last week empty-handed. I've had a team put together some proposals as to possible further actions."

Ella pulled a tablet out of her briefcase and touched its surface, prompting it to synch with a halo-projector in the center of the conference table. A holographic plan appeared, floating in the air.

Robert stood up abruptly and swatted it away. "With all due respect, Ella, it's been ten years since we've heard anything from James or his crew and twenty since he's sat in this room. We all know they're dead. It's time to cut our losses and move on."

Ella could scarcely believe what she was hearing. Her cheeks started to burn red.

"You've been a fine interim CEO," Robert went on duplicitously, "but what we really need is a career professional. Someone who can move us forward and take us to the next level."

Ella stood up. She wanted to reach across the table and gouge out Robert's eyes with her bare hands, but she strived to overcome her baser instincts and remain calm and collected. "Cut our losses?" she said, eyebrows raised. "This is James Odysseus we're talking about. When he inherited this company from his father, it was little more than a fly-by-night operation. James built this company from the ground up! He handpicked each and every one of you. There is no one more qualified to run this company than him."

Ella's eyes narrowed. She looked around the room at the board members, feeling their almost-palpable thirst for profits. She knew her control of the situation was slipping out from under her.

"We understand how much he meant to you," Vince interrupted. "The way you've championed him steadfastly all these years speaks highly of your character—other wives would have moved on."

Ella pressed her lips together. It irked her to no end that they still saw her merely as "the wife." Had she not helmed the company successfully for the past twenty years? She had more experience— albeit accidentally—than the top three Fortune 500 CEOs combined. She wondered quietly to herself when backhanded sexism would die.

"We all miss him, Ella, but James is gone," Vince continued. "The company is still here, and we need new leadership."

Ella took a deep breath, realizing she should stop while she was ahead – the board meeting had just started and would continue a few hours minimum. She dreaded these formal gatherings, it was painful listening to these old boorish men, who loved to hear the sound of their own voices. Strategically, she continued with the other necessary board agenda items.

As soon as possible, two hours later, she wrapped up the meeting. "As I have stated before, when Project Loom is complete, the company will be well positioned to take on a new CEO. We've made some significant progress, and we are in the homestretch. I'll leave you with the quarterly report to review. Let's call this meeting to adjourn so that I can get to running the company." She aimed that last remark squarely at Vince and Robert.

The secretary passed around tablets with the report updating the progress on Project Loom as Ella left the room.

After glancing briefly at the reports, the eight board members resumed eating gluttonously, drinking excessively, and bantering like old friends. Another assortment of post-board meeting delicacies was served: rosemary rack of lamb, lobster bisque, truffle soufflés, and escargot were ceremoniously presented on silver platters. Wine pairings of exquisite French and Italian old-vine reserves were poured into vintage crystal goblets.

Vince slipped out of the room and followed Ella. He grabbed her by the wrist as she was about to round a corner. "Ella, I hope you've given some thought to what I said the other day." He reached up with his free hand and swept her hair out of her eyes.

Ella was partially flattered and partially disgusted by Vince's advances. It had been so long since James had left… She was starting to feel her age catch up with her. With the advances in medicine, gene modification, and personal care, over the past century, it was quite common for Earthlings to look youthful into their fifties. However, even a confident woman like Ella, at times felt insecure. Occasionally, she questioned whether she was even attractive anymore. Had she lost her good looks?

Despite her own better judgment, Ella felt momentarily tempted by Vince. He was tall, with sandy blonde hair speckled with gray. He had been at Gordonstoun the same year James was, and afterwards, they had remained good friends. Vince had even been one of James' first appointed board members. However, ever since James had gone missing, Ella had noticed Vince jockeying for power, manipulating the other board members, and profiting from sweetheart deals. She might have been attracted to Vince had it not been for his moral turpitude.

"On your own," Vince said, "the board will never accept you as CEO. If we partnered together, though, I'd have the appearance of power, but really I'd be your protector, your champion. You would run the company through me. I'd be the head, but you would be the neck. I'd turn whichever way pleased you."

She could see the logic in his thinking—she probably would be better off partnered with a strong, charismatic leader like Vince. But she couldn't give up on James. It just wasn't in her to walk away not knowing what had become of him. She would never forgive herself if she moved on too soon.

"I'm just not ready, Vince," she told him. "Besides, you're an old friend. We have too much history to start anything new."

But Vince was never one to take a hint. He moved in closer, wrapping his arm around Ella's waist. "You and me together, we'd be unstoppable," he said urgently. "We'd usher in a new era for this company! Besides that, I know you've thought about it." His eyes ran up and down her sleek figure.

"Oh, grow up!" Ella replied as she pushed him away.

Vince glanced around, then leaned in and stuck his tongue halfway down her throat.

She slapped him across the face and wiped his wet sloppy kiss on her sleeve. "Fuck off, Vince!" she barked as she stormed away.

Vince took that as a first refusal in a series of feminine games that would lead up to an eventual acceptance of his advances. He turned, heading back to the conference room and smiling to himself as he thought about the next move he would use to get into Ella's pants.

Ella brushed herself off and stepped into the lab where her researchers were working on Project Loom. She was an expert at compartmentalizing, and she refused to let him ruin her day. She turned her focus away from the thought of his slimy mouth on hers and let the abhorrent feeling of being cornered float out of her mind.

Feeling more like her normal confident and amiable self, she went about checking in with her design team. A board showing images of the Loom clothing design details took up most of one of the walls. It was smart clothing that diagnosed, sealed off, and treated injuries: there were pictures of skiers wearing sleek Loom sportswear as they jumped out of eagle vehicles onto snowy mountaintops, a picture of a surfer in a Loom wetsuit cresting a 30-meter wave, and an image of a paraglider wearing a Loom jacket as she soared 500 meters up in the air over a rocky beach. Project Loom was Ella's personal project, and she was proud of their sleek designs and significant progress.

Ella meticulously made her rounds through the workspace, checking in with each engineer. She knew them all by name, and she knew about their families and personal struggles. Her team had become her family—she did everything she could to support and look after them.

At Jane's desk, Ella leaned over and made a few minor adjustments. "The design should hug a little tighter here," she said, pointing. "If we can successfully infuse that spider DNA thread we isolated last week into the fabric, it will be stronger and better able to withstand trauma." She took a half-step back. "Where are we at with the bark spider DNA sequencing?"

Jane slumped a little in her chair. "There was a hack last night—someone logged into the system, downloaded a month's worth of updates from the cloud, and then purged the files, probably to cover their tracks. This is a huge setback."

"Not again!" Ella exclaimed. She looked genuinely distraught. "That's the third time this year! Pallas, page security. Let's see what they can find out." She realized that everyone else in the room was listening to their conversation.

"Everyone, back to work," she said loudly. "The board is on my case to finish this project ASAP, and I know you've all put your hearts and souls into this. I want you to know that I appreciate your efforts! Let's keep it up. We're in the homestretch."

She scanned the room for responses. Most of her team had been with her for years. They were all extremely loyal, smart, hardworking, and dedicated. But they also had the emotional nuance to know not to ask too many questions regarding this project and its delays.

Ella stepped into her corner office and closed the door. She checked to make sure no one was looking, then exhaled a sigh of relief and sank into her chair. She was naturally a straightforward and forthcoming person who didn't like hiding things from her team. As the interim CEO, however, she had learned to do what was needed, even when sometimes what was required didn't feel right to her.

She could hear James' voice in her head: "The ends justify the means." It was a phrase she had once hated, but she had recently come to rely on it more and more to keep her moving forward.

Ella touched a button on her desk. It confirmed her DNA, and then a halo screen appeared in front of her. A message popped up that she opened with a flick of a finger.

Michael appeared. He looked as though he were around 50 himself—a few fine lines creased his forehead, and a blast of white streaked his black hair. He was dressed in a Chinese shirt that was typical business attire in the Asian Union. When he spoke, he spoke in Mandarin. "Ella, I need to talk with you in person. It's imperative that you come see me right away."

It had been years since Ella had seen or even heard from Michael. What could be so important that he had to speak to her in person? She knew he was not one to make such a request lightly. Still, she didn't feel like she could get away at the moment—the board might take advantage of her absence and call an emergency meeting to file a motion to replace her.

Just then, Max appeared in the doorway, and Ella swiped the halo screen away. "Brought your favorite! Seaweed brown rice rolls," Max said, holding up a bag from home.

"You made lunch—how sweet!" Ella exclaimed as she stood up and helped Max lay out the meal on her desk.

"Well, actually, Hestia made it," he admitted. "You were up early!" He sat down in the chair across the desk from her.

Ella sighed. "There was a board meeting."

"They're pushing you to make your recommendation for a new CEO?" Max guessed.

"Yes, but I don't know… I just have this feeling that James is still out there." Ella looked away from Max and at the window, hoping her son wouldn't see the tears welling up in her eyes. A familiar pain shot through her chest and stung the corners of her nostrils. It was the feeling of loss, of wanting to hold on and fearing letting go too soon. It stung her to the core. Normally, Ella was emotionally impenetrable, but when she was with her son, she let down her guard.

"It's been ten years since anyone's heard from him," Max said gently. "I'm the last person to want to tell you this, Mom, but it is time to move on."

Ella put down her food. "I have a favor to ask you," she said, regaining her composure. "Remember Dad's friend from school, Michael? He said he needs to speak with me in person. Given everything that's going on here, I really can't get away. Can you go for me? I know he'd love to see you."

Max could barely remember Michael, but he knew Michael was partially responsible for his father's involvement in Project Stella. "Ahhh… I don't know," he said hesitantly.

"Please?" Ella pleaded with a pout.

"Okay, sure, Mom," Max said after another moment.

Ella smiled, feeling victorious. She went back to enjoying her lunch with a newfound vigor.

Max poked at his food, but still, he was pleased to see that his mother was happy.

CHAPTER 3

MAX

The last time Max had seen Michael was also the last time he had seen his father. Max had only been two at the time, and all he could remember was hearing shouting and arguing between the two men. Max had wiggled his way out of his mother's arms and run head-long between his father and his friend, thinking he could stop the fight. If he concentrated, Max could still remember the feeling of hot tears pouring down his cheeks as he begged his father to stop shouting, reaching up with outstretched arms and hoping to get picked up and swooped away. James had indeed picked up Max, but only to hand him off to his mother. Then he had resumed his argument with Michael.

There was no way Max could have known they were arguing about the voyage that would keep his father away for twenty years and possibly cost him his life. Had he known, Max would have begged his father not to leave. Nothing was worth the loss of time together.

James had essentially missed Max's entire childhood. When Max was five, he had started keeping a holographic journal of all his special moments to share with his father when he returned. Birthdays, class presentations, athletic triumphs… Max recorded little snippets of his life, saving them, hoping to one day share all of the milestones he had missed with his father.

As the years went on, Max recorded entries less and less frequently. One day, he stopped altogether, assuming that James was lost; he resigned himself to the fact that his father would never return. But he kept the little holographic log near his bedside table, and late at night when he couldn't sleep, Max would scroll through the journal entries, imagining that his father was sitting next to him with his arm wrapped around his shoulder, sharing these moments with him. Somehow, his little ritual always had the desired effect of calming Max down, centering him, and making him feel safe and sleepy. After a few minutes of this meditative activity, Max would close his eyes and drift off to sleep.

Lying in bed, Max often imagined how his life would one day be different. It would be better—nothing like his lonely childhood. He saw his future self grown and married, living in a warm, loving house filled with laughter and joy. His son and daughter were playing on the floor with their toys; his grandparents were visiting and playing with the kids while he prepared a holiday meal. Old-fashioned jazz music hummed in the background. Everyone would be happy and joyful, and singing and laughter would fill the house.

Then he would open his eyes and listen to the quiet of his almost-empty home, a place where humans were outnumbered by AI. While their tree house was comfortable enough, ever since his father had left, it had felt empty and lonely.

As Max became a teenager, he learned more about his father and the business that had taken him so far away. Michael and James had both invested in and made technological contributions to Project Stella as part of an intergalactic group of scientists and corporations that had banded together to harvest matter from two massive black holes orbiting one another. Stella's technology then transported the incredibly dense matter from the black holes to a chosen star in the galaxy. Using Stella's complex AI programming, the group was able to harness that energy to design and create a planet to fit the requirements of a client—should a client want a planet with a higher composition of H2O or a planet rich in iron or gold, Stella could theoretically make a planet to suit those particular requirements that would then orbit the chosen star.

It was a game-changer for the intergalactic community. Each member of the organization that had joined forces to create Stella signed a treaty to defend and protect the technology against any party that might try to steal or corrupt it for their own purposes. The members of the treaty called themselves the Stellaes.

One of the first potential clients were the Hectarans. Whereas Earth had chosen to embrace biological sciences and green technologies 200 years ago, thus stemming the damage of global warming, the Hectarans had refused to change their carbon footprint. Consequently, they had destroyed their home planet beyond repair and rendered it uninhabitable. Those who could buy or trade for a place on a starship survived, but most of those left behind died of disasters directly caused by climate change: famine, drought, fires, typhoons, and earthquakes, among other catastrophes. The majority of the surviving Hectarans made a new home onboard a massive spherical spaceship they called New Hectar.

Paran was an eminent Hectaran scientist who visited Project Stella. He was so impressed and inspired by what he saw that he became consumed with the idea of recreating the Hectaran home world. When the Hectarans lost their bid for the first pilot planet to a well-to-do corporate competitor, Paran fumed in private and plotted to take what he felt he and his fellow remaining Hectarans deserved. One night while the science teams were hosting a tech conference, Paran stole Stella and took the prototype to the Hectaran home spaceship.

Some on New Hectar wanted to send Paran and Stella back. Others—including those in power—sided with Paran. Inspired by his dream of recreating the Hectaran home world, Hectaran politicians sold the public on the idea of "Hectar 2." What they didn't realize was that in stealing Stella, Paran had unwittingly invoked a clause of the Stellaes treaty that called upon all of the Stellaes to defend the technology and retrieve Stella. James was one of the Stellae members.

When James first learned that Stella had been taken, he tried to shirk his responsibilities. After all, he was merely a scientist and a businessman—what did he know of space travel and war? Most of all, James abhorred the idea of being separated from his wife and young son. He loved his happy home life with Ella and Max. In the end, though, when threatened with a crippling legal battle that would undoubtedly dissolve his company, he reluctantly agreed to fulfill his contractual obligations. He could never have imagined it would cost him so much.

Max still wished he could turn back time and beg his father not to go. Or perhaps he could have been a stowaway on the ship so that he could have faced the dangers of space alongside his father even though he thought it was pointless to fight a war on the other side of the galaxy.

Max had mixed feelings about going to visit Michael. Yes, Michael had been one of his father's best friends…but Max also believed that Michael was the reason why his father had missed all of his birthdays, all of his school plays, all of his sporting events. Logically, Max knew it wasn't really Michael's fault, but still, he couldn't help resenting the fact that Michael had returned safely with his crew while his father was nowhere to be found.

Max packed a small bag of essentials and loaded it into his eagle vehicle. "Set a course for the Asian Union, destination Michael's residence," Max said as the vehicle buckled him in.

"Setting course. Estimated travel time is 12 hours and 34 minutes." As the vehicle lifted off and swooped through the air, Max felt his stomach start to twist. Although counterbalancing motion helped keep the ride as smooth as possible, even experienced drivers often felt motion sickness on takeoff and landing, and Max tended to get motion sickness easily. That was another reason he had been hesitant to take on this task.

"Initiate auto pilot, then bring up everything you can find on Michael," Max said, fidgeting with his tablet to distract himself. A screen appeared, and images and text filtered in as the computer scoured photo libraries, social media, and news articles for related material. Max used the flight time to read about his father's old friend.

Max saw old pictures of Michael, his father, his mother, and a few other friends hanging out at university. They all seemed so young and carefree! Two hours into the flight, Max discovered that Michael had had a falling-out with his older brother, Andrew, during the war with Hectar. Andrew—who had also invested in Project Stella—was the driving party behind the war. He was the first to enforce the treaty, and he had been the dominant player in strong-arming the other parties into bringing back Stella. Andrew claimed to be supporting Michael, a scientist practically married to his life's work. However, it was clear from the news coverage that Michael had felt that Andrew was taking advantage of the situation, profiting from the war through his weapons and security businesses. The greater the cost of war, the more Andrew profited.

Michael was one of the leading astrophysicists in the galaxy. Whereas Andrew had been a successful corporate tycoon, Michael was a brilliant academic. He was the lead designer of Project Stella, the mastermind behind its initial concept and technological designs. He spent so much time designing Stella that he had even joked Stella was his "true love." Of course he wanted to get Stella back, but not at the cost of human lives. He abhorred the death and destruction caused by the war.

Max's eyes started to feel heavy, so he leaned back to rest for a moment. He nodded off. Time seemed to blur together in a foggy forgetfulness. He woke, suddenly, to the computer's announcement: "Arriving at Michael's residence in five minutes."

Damn it! he thought. *I had so much more that I wanted to read up on before this visit. I must have slept for eight hours.* Max wiped the dried drool off the side of his mouth and ran his hands through his disheveled hair. While he could get away with rolling out of bed and throwing on a t-shirt in the EU, the AU was more formal, and Max worried momentarily that he might be judged by his shabby appearance.

The eagle vehicle flew steadily over lush, green rice fields. Jagged mountains in the distance cast their mirror images into still lakes. At the base of one of the mountains sat a beautifully manicured Chinese garden with koi ponds, bridges, flowering trees, cranes, and cormorant birds tied to android fishermen who doubled as gardeners. A massive tree compound three times the size of James' house sat in perfect harmony with its surroundings—the trees that grew together to form the building were an Asian species similar to bonsai, and the mansion appeared to fit naturally into the mountain setting. The compound boasted four wings and had a central courtyard garden in its center, where a flowering tree shaded an old stone bench. Petals were blowing in the wind, falling like tiny, pale-butterfly-wing snowflakes.

Max's eagle vehicle landed in front of the central entrance. He stepped out, doing his best to brush off his slightly wrinkled clothes, then pulled a small box of chocolates out of his bag and headed for the door. The immensity of the house was rather intimidating; Max was painfully aware of his insignificance in comparison to the grandiose door. When he touched it, the computer scanned his face and a bell rang throughout the house. The sound chimed down the halls and disappeared into the velvety living walls.

The branches parted, and Michael appeared on the other side. Michael beamed with joy at seeing the son of his old friend. He greeted Max in Mandarin. Ever since the merging of the major continental unions, Mandarin had been the official language of the Asian Union and English had been the most widely used language in the European Union. The majority of educated humans spoke both, however, and Mandarin had become slightly more dominant in the last century.

"Max, you're all grown up! I remember when you were this high," Michael said, gesturing to the height of his knees.

"Uncle Michael!" Max said, greeting Michael with the polite term "uncle" that he used with all of his parent's friends in the Asian Union. "So nice to see you! It's been too long. These are for you from my mother." Max handed Michael the box of chocolates, surprised by his own feelings of joy at seeing Michael. Perhaps it was Michael's contagious grin, his outstretched arms, or his earnest desire to assist his friend's only son... Whatever the reason, despite his former musings about his father's friend, Max let a feeling of happiness overtake him.

"Thank you," Michael said, accepting the box. "Come on in! You must be tired from your flight. Can I get you anything?" He ushered Max through the door and started showing him around.

They entered a large room that led to a massive formal sitting area decorated with a mixture of classical Chinese and modern Asian Union décor. "Windows open," Michael said, and the intertwined window shutters opened, letting in a gust of fresh air and sunlight.

An android brought in some hot tea and moon cakes. "You've arrived just in time for the autumn moon festival," Michael said. "Tonight you'll see the moon pass at its closest proximity to the Earth in its annual rotation—it will appear especially large and bright when it rises and sets." He poured their tea, holding back his sleeve with the other hand. Steam swirled out of the teapot's spout.

Max was rather distracted by the scale of the room—it made him feel smaller and more childlike than usual. He had come to think of himself as a grown man, but suddenly, as he sat with his father's friend, Max felt tiny and insignificant. He lost his normal eloquence.

There was a long and awkward pause in the conversation; the sound they made as they sipped the fragrant chrysanthemum tea seemed to echo through the oversized room. Max struggled to get out a simple sentence and finally succeeded. "What was he like? My father, I mean." Relieved that it was no longer his turn to talk, Max relaxed a little and studied Michael's features, trying to see if he could guess any details about his character.

Michael carefully set down his teacup before answering. "In school," he finally said, "James was always the most clever and cunning. He never needed to study, and he was always up to something." Michael chuckled a little as he remembered his old friend. "One time the dean came back and found his eagle vehicle parked in his office. We never figured out how James pulled off that prank." Michael shook his head and took another sip of tea.

Max laughed at the notion of his father being a mischievous schoolboy. He had grown up imagining his father as a model citizen, upright and stoic. This new mischievous and playful account of his father made his insides tickle a little.

Michael continued, "You know, we probably owe our lives to him—he came up with the plan that ended the war. Otherwise, we might still be there, or dead."

They both lapsed into silence, but then Max decided to address the main purpose of the visit. "You said you needed to speak to my mother? She apologizes that she couldn't get away, but she sends her regards."

"Yes, I thought it might be hard for Ella to get away what with the board tightening the noose around the neck of your company." Michael put down his teacup again. "That's why I couldn't send this over a transmission—you never know who might intercept it and what they might do with the information," he said with a wink.

He walked over to his desk and pressed a button, prompting his halo screen to pop up. "Pallas, play James' transmission."

A scratchy image flickered into view. It was a blurry image of a shaggy, dirty James coming in and out of focus. "If you're receiving this message," said his image, "tell my family that I'm okay. I've been trapped on a moon of a gas giant orbiting Lenara for the past seven years. I think I've just fixed my escape pod's thrusters and will be able to—" The transmission broke up.

Max's heart skipped a beat. "Lenara??" he gasped. "That's fifteen thousand light years away! He'll never make it home in an escape pod!" Max was worried and excited at the same time. Unlike Ella, he had long ago given up on the idea that his father might still be alive, but seeing his father's fuzzy image gave him newfound hope. *Mom's right—he might still be out there!* he thought eagerly. Yet at the same time, he also knew the odds were against his father ever making it home.

Although Michael had his own doubts, he harbored hope, too, and now he tried to reassure Max. "Based on its time stamp, it looks like the message took a year to get here, and given that the transmission is so grainy, his ship and communications must have been badly damaged," he said as he handed Max a small storage drive with a copy of the transmission. Despite his words, he was grinning. "But your father is the most resourceful rascal I know—he'll find a way to get back."

Max took the storage drive wordlessly, still caught between hope and despair.

Michael patted his shoulder. "For all you know, your father might already be close to home! I contacted friends in a nearby region to do a sweep of that moon. They said they'll let me know if they find anything."

The inside of Max's nose burned as tears started to well up in his eyes. He swatted them away with his sleeve. "Thank you, Uncle Michael!" he said. "We owe you a great debt."

"Not at all! If it weren't for your father, we might have all perished out there in that dark hellhole." Michael briefly put an arm around Max. "Stay here tonight, then get back to your mother and let her know that your father is coming home."

CHAPTER 4

PROJECT LOOM

24 hours earlier…

The office was dark. The engineers, administrative staff, and executives had gone home several hours before. A lone security guard made his rounds sluggishly as he sipped lukewarm coffee, trying to stay alert. His eyes felt heavy; reluctantly and against his own better judgment, he sat down on a large couch in an executive's office and unwittingly nodded off.

Down a long corridor, a sleek shadow-like figure silently opened a window and slipped into the office unnoticed, landing quietly and softly. Through the window, the moon cast a pool of cool white light against the textured tree-walls. The figure moved swiftly through the hallways, heading straight to Project Loom's workspace. Wasting no time, the person set to work hacking into the mainframe. Files started downloading to an offshore server. After being downloaded, they were deleted permanently off the mainframe.

Although she had done this several times before, each time she did it, she felt as though the loud thumping in her chest might cause her heart to explode. She was acutely aware of the sound of her breath in the dead quiet of the room. Every moment waiting for the files to download felt like an eternity. Was it possible that they wouldn't download while she was looking at them? She tried watching the door instead, but didn't seem to make the process go any faster. Finally, though, her task was complete. She turned everything off and made it look as though she had never been there.

She exited the same way she had come: down the corridor, out the window, down the side of the building, and across the street. Relieved to be out of the building, she let out an audible sigh of relief. Her heart rate slowed back to normal, but she couldn't shake the anxious jittery feeling crawling on her skin.

After walking a long distance, she removed her light-absorbing shell jacket and turned it inside-out to reveal a green coat. She pulled her hair out of a ponytail and shook out her long auburn waves. Feeling grateful that things had gone according to plan, Ella rounded another corner, checking several times to make sure she hadn't been followed.

I seem to be getting good at this, she thought ruefully. She was a little sad that she was becoming a talented vandal. Although she had broken in and deleted files several times, each time had felt like it would be her last. *I'll send out a private search party, and we'll find James. This will be the last time*, she'd think after each break-in.

A small patch of brush led into a denser collection of trees. Ella made her way through them without so much as the crunch of a single leaf underfoot. *All those years of ballet training she'd had in childhood were finally good for something*, she mused to herself.

She had been a very talented dancer, and Ella was a little sad when she gave it up to focus more on her schoolwork. As the years passed, she discovered with very little effort, she continued to maintain her flexibility and agility. She'd practice tendus and arabesques in the bathroom while brushing her teeth, and later picked up Wushu as a hobby. She also had a particular aptitude for stealth, she knew. Her feet melted into the ground, toes first, one step at a time.

In the darkest part of the bush, she retrieved her eagle vehicle. Slipping into it, she quietly started the computer and soared up silently into the night.

As she flew over the island, she saw the familiar places she had visited so many times over the years. There was the dirt path she used to walk along hand-in-hand with James on their way to the rocky beach below. In the pale light of the moon, she saw her favorite cove, the one where she had taught Max to swim so many years ago.

It was hard to reconcile the many sides of herself—she had become so many versions of herself to so many people. She knew deep down that she was a good person. She was a mother, a friend, and a confidant, someone people could rely on. But out of necessity, she had also become hard, reserved, and withdrawn. She had closed off parts of herself within an internal labyrinth and thrown away the key. Over time, weeds had grown over the entryway, and there was no one left who remembered the location of the entrance. She boxed secrets within secrets and wondered if it was even possible for anyone to really "know" her anymore.

Some secrets, she felt, were better kept secret. Probably best if she took them with her to the grave.

Project Loom had become her baby. It was her pet project and often her raison d'être. It was also her sole stalling tactic and the reason the company had not yet been overtaken by the board. Each time she snuck in to unravel the work she had already done, it pained her to destroy it, yet sabotaging Project Loom on a regular basis was a necessity. She needed more time as the interim CEO!

Fortunately, she had gotten the board to agree to hold off making any top-level management decisions until they launched their new product. They had only agreed to do so because they saw the inherent value of the project and the potential it had to increase shareholder value. It could even be its own standalone company one day.

The halo screen in her eagle vehicle showed her the latest news about the fire that had popped up on the west coast of the African Union. The EU had sent in firefighting equipment to help the AU— several thousand atmospheric drones had been placed along the coast to heat up and evaporate water, and another thousand fan drones were guiding the precipitation towards the fire. The authorities believed they'd have it put out by sunrise.

Ella found natural disasters to be the perfect opportunity to sneak into the office unnoticed. When everyone was consumed with major disasters, who would notice her coming and going?

After landing at home, Ella sat in the vehicle for a long while. She looked up at the stars, wondering where James might be in the immense void of space. Maybe at this very moment, he was also looking at the same twinkling points of light. The veins in her nose began to tingle and her eyes started to moisten. She silently snuck back into the house without arousing any suspicion and went back to bed.

CHAPTER 5:

JAMES

One year ago...

Lying on the ground, head buried under a disassembled computer panel, James was connecting multicolored wires inside the escape pod. The lights turned on. This was the first time the power had come back on in years. Trying not to feel overly optimistic, James said, "Run diagnostics."

The computer replied, "Forward thrusters are 25%. Fuel is 12%. Solar energy is 30%."

James let out a joyful yell, fists pumping the air.

After a moment, fearing that he might jinx this momentary spell of good luck, James refocused his attention on the task at hand. "Open Hermes, prepare an internal transmission, and set a course for Ectara," he said aloud. A slew of tearful and heartfelt messages that he wanted to say to his loved ones passed through his mind. However, given the distance from his current location to Earth and the condition of the pod, James knew there was a good chance that the message would never make it to them—or if it did, it might first pass through the hands of several distant acquaintances.

James decided to record a to-the-point halo message and send it through the Stellaes transmission system, Hermes, to any Stellaes on Earth who might be able to receive it.

After recording and sending his message, James looked out the window at the cloudy sky. Silently, he prayed his message would be delivered safely to Earth and find its way to his family.

"Pallas, lift off," he said. He braced for a rocky ascent. Given that the pod had been stranded on this desolate hunk of dirt for seven years, he was not even sure they would make it out of the moon's gravitational force—there was a good chance the pod would come apart at the seams. In a way, he wished his spacecraft would blow up on takeoff. At least that would put an end to his long, drawn-out misery.

For the past seven years, James had asked himself over and over again, "Why did I survive when all the rest of my men perished?" The guilt had been eating away at him. Had life not been such a terrible, solitary, and bleak existence of scarcely surviving, the remorse might have killed him. However, James had been too miserable trying to recharge his solar batteries, repair his pod, and find sustenance to wallow in his losses.

"Confirming coordinates and plotting route," the computer informed him right before lifting off. The pod bumped along as it soared out of the atmosphere.

Once in space, the ride smoothed out. "Preparing to warp in 10, 9, 8, 7, 6, 5, 4, 3, 2, 1…"

The pod jumped into warp; the stars melted away into long streaks of light slowly streaming past James' ship.

"Estimated travel time is 4 hours and 22 minutes."

James relaxed a little. "Pallas, open hologram video of Ella and Max." Ever since his computer had turned itself off to conserve energy, James had not seen a video or image of his family in years, and gradually, his memories of them had started to fade. Perhaps the prolonged isolation had exacerbated the problem, but it hurt more than anything to feel as though he were losing his memories of his beloved wife and son. Some years back, James had realized that he couldn't see the faces of his friends and family in his mind anymore, just blurry images he associated with their memories.

A crisp holographic video of Ella holding a birthday cake appeared, floating in the air before him. James sighed, relieved to see her clearly once again. All of his fears were displaced now that he could clearly recall his loved ones. Ella brought the cake, alight with candles, to a beaming Max, who promptly blew them out.

James leaned back in his chair and closed his eyes. As he started to doze off, he heard a loud crack. One of the side panels of the pod had split apart! He rushed to it, grabbed both sides of the crack, and held it together with his hands.

Frantically, he looked around the pod for his laser tool, but it was just out of reach. "Dammit!" he said aloud. "Just my luck! I finally get back in space, and the damn pod splits apart at the seams."

Inspiration struck. "Pallas, cancel gravitational balance!" he commanded.

"Canceling gravitational balance."

Seconds later, items were floating around the pod. James felt his own body start to lift off of the floor. As he had hoped it would, the laser tool began to drift towards him. James poked at it with his foot, hooking it in his general direction. As it floated closer, he caught it between his legs. Using his body and one arm to hold the panel together, he grasped the laser tool in his other hand and hastily soldered the panel, melting the metal together at the seams.

He told the computer to reinstate gravitational balance and almost slumped onto the floor in relief. A few minutes later, he recovered enough to go stand at the window and look out at the stars streaming by as the pod kept moving at warp speed.

Four hours later, the pod jumped out of warp. A mostly blue planet with a few small green land masses floated like a jewel in space. "Pallas, bring the pod in for a landing close to the capital," James said. He made sure he was firmly strapped into his chair in case the landing didn't go smoothly.

His precaution was warranted. "Affirmative," the computer replied, bringing the sputtering pod to land on Ectara. It circled the mostly blue-green planet and came in for a rocky landing, nearly burning up as it passed through the atmosphere on its way down. The pod crashed into a meadow.

Dazed, James managed to unhook himself from his chair. He grabbed a small sack of emergency supplies and stumbled out of the pod and into the tall grass, getting away from the flames as fast as he could. He ran, tripped over a tree root, and fell to the ground. Behind him, he heard a loud *boom!* and glanced over his shoulder to see that he had barely escaped in time to see the pod explode. He rolled over in the grass and looked up at the clear blue sky, wiping sweat, blood, and soot away from his face.

James closed his eyes and listened to the hypnotic melody of insects hissing and birds chirping. He couldn't quite decide if the birds sounded cheerful and happy or if he were hearing a vicious war song between rival birds fighting over mates. Far off in the distance, he heard the faint sound of water running over rocks.

He opened his eyes and watched a few clouds drift across a mostly blue sky. For a moment, he wondered how there could be such a beautiful and peaceful place while so much death, destruction, and misery could be going on somewhere else in the universe.

Emotional and physical exhaustion kept him pinned to the ground for some time. His body felt heavy, as though it were sinking into the damp earth. Eventually, he took a deep breath, pushed himself up, collected his sack, and walked towards the edge of the tree line.

Following the sound of the running water led James to discover a stream meandering through the forest. He knelt in the shade of the old trees and retrieved his compact water bottle from his sack. After elongating the bottle, he filled it with water from the stream, watching as it dripped through a series of filters, purifying and cleansing the fluid. After a long moment, he was able to take a deep, satisfying sip. As he wiped his mouth on his sleeve, James heard the giggling and shrieking of girls faintly in the distance. With a shrug—where else did he have to go?—he decided to follow the sound of their voices.

Eventually, the stream became a cascading waterfall; he kept following it and saw that its path ended in a large pool. Through the trees, he glimpsed a group of young humanoid women swimming, laughing as they took turns jumping off rocks into the cool water.

One of them caught sight of James through the trees and shrieked. Startled, they hurried to get out of the water and cover themselves.

Another girl stepped forward. "Who's there?" she shouted.

James moved slowly into view. With his soiled clothes and messy, overgrown hair, he looked like a wild cave man. However, despite his rugged appearance, the girl apparently noticed that his intelligent blue eyes conveyed a hint of his true self.

"My name is James Odysseus, and my ship crashed over there in that meadow just beyond the forest," James said slowly and carefully, gesturing in the general direction of the meadow as he spoke. He thought he could almost detect the very faint scent of a burning spacecraft if he concentrated hard enough…but no, he had crashed a long ways off. He must be imagining it or losing his mind.

The girl didn't say anything right away in response, so James simply maintained eye contact and assessed the situation. She appeared to be in her late twenties, he decided, with long, damp blonde hair that fell almost to her waist. She seemed empathetic, stern, and powerful all at the same time.

For her part, she was trying to decide what she thought of James. When her initial shock had passed, despite her better judgment, she was curious to find out more about him. She decided to offer him her assistance. "I'm sorry to hear that," she finally said, taking a step closer. "That's very unfortunate."

"No kidding," James replied. Her friends giggled a little.

She approached James slowly, as one might hesitantly move closer to a wild animal. She stepped back towards the edge of the water and then through it, walking towards James, her bathing gown floating in her wake.

"May I?" she asked when she reached him.

James lowered his head. As he closed his eyes, he felt her long, delicate fingers brush his rough hair away from his face, smoothing out the tangles. Although he had only just met her, through her touch, James felt as though he had known her before; he felt as if he recognized her soul. He opened his eyes and searched her green ones for some sign of recognition.

She was still trying to make up her mind about James as well, he could see. "Swim with us," she told him. "My attendants will bathe you."

James looked at her attendants. They were young, pretty girls, with pleasant if not complaisant demeanors.

It didn't take him long to agree. He hadn't had a proper bath in seven years! Quickly, he stepped into the cool fresh water, and the attendants removed his soiled clothes. He dunked his shoulders, neck, and head under the water a few times. One of the girls washed his face with a damp cloth, wiping away the soot and grime. Another used a handful of small purple flowers to lather his hair before she waved him towards the waterfall where he could rinse himself. It felt so amazingly wonderful to be clean again! The cold water was miraculously refreshing.

Next, they proceeded to trim his beard and hair, carefully cutting away the matted hair from his face and head. Their hands felt soft and gentle against his skin. Finally, they dressed him in a long cloth garment that folded over one shoulder and cascaded down his back. He practically felt like a new person.

The girls smiled at their handiwork. "Much better," the one who had spoken to him said. She was obviously pleased with his transformation. "Follow me."

James had no idea where he was going, but he assumed he'd find out soon enough. Besides, what other option did he have? The girls started walking through the forest, and James followed.

"I'll show you the way to the city," the blonde girl told him. "Then you can announce yourself to the high council at sunset. They are having a celebration this evening, and it is customary to welcome wayward travelers. My father and mother will help you." She stopped to pin a wildflower on a fold of his garment.

"And who are you?" James inquired.

The girls giggled again, but hushed their laughter when James tilted his head slightly and gave them a quizzical look.

"Deleanaa, princess of Ectara," his savior replied.

James' eyebrows went up, and he bowed slightly.

"No need for that!" Deleanaa said, lifting his chin with her hand. She much preferred meeting someone new in this unusual way. Most people treated her so formally! It was refreshing to talk with a stranger as any ordinary person might.

Fortunately for Deleanaa, James was not easily swayed by social status or rank, and he continued to treat her as he had before: with a mixture of polite curiosity and straightforward charm.

The attendants walked on ahead as Deleanaa and James talked. Deleanaa told James about Ectara, and James told Deleanaa about Earth and his troubles in returning home. They compared notes about how the inhabitants of both planets had turned the tides of global warming and found sustainable sources of energy. Whereas humans had developed new biological technologies that had reversed Earth's carbon footprint and made manufacturing eco-friendly, the Ectarans had long ago developed a multitude of crystalline technologies, she told him. They used their crystal-based technologies to manufacture cities and construction materials, store solar energy, and develop various information technologies and art forms.

James was so fascinated with their conversation that he didn't see a low-hanging branch along the path and walked right into it, badly bruising his left temple. From then on, he was more careful to avoid wayward trees. Deleanaa didn't repeat his mistake, but from time to time, she lost her balance and steadied herself on his arm as they walked across slippery rocks.

The most harrowing part of the journey—at least, for James— came when they had to cross a long, narrow crystal bridge that connected two cliffs. When they reached it, James paused for a while at the edge of the bridge. He wasn't altogether sure that the delicate structure would support his weight.

"Don't worry," Deleanaa said. "It's stronger than it looks—it's been here for a thousand years and will probably last for a thousand more."

That failed to make James feel any more sure about the bridge's safety. Ahead of them, the girls sped along unconcerned; they had crossed this bridge hundreds of times. Every time James glanced down, though, he felt weak in the knees. In fact, when he looked through the delicate, transparent surface of the bridge and down the great distance to the forest floor below, he thought he might pass out. Still, he had no choice but to take a step onto the bridge at Deleanaa's urging.

The crossing seemed to go on forever, but in reality, it only lasted for a matter of minutes. It felt like an eternity to James, though, and he was relieved when he made it across to solid ground. On the other side of the bridge, the forest continued for another hundred meters or so, at which point they emerged from the shadows of the forest and into the light of the afternoon sun.

Far off in the distance, the ocean met a rocky beach. The beach turned into a steep cliff that rose into a series of hills and valleys; on the edge of the hill was a beautiful gleaming city made of crystal buildings that shimmered in the daylight. Its beauty was almost blinding.

Deleanaa stopped for a moment and looked out at the large metropolis of tall crystal buildings resting at the edge of the sea. "Behold Ectara City," she said, smiling at him. "Is it not just as I've described? Remember, when the sun sets over the water tonight, the new year's festivities will begin."

James was still staring at the crystal city as she kept talking. "Follow the main bridge into the city," she instructed. "At the end of it, you will find the castle. Announce yourself in the great hall—my parents will assist you." She reached out and lightly squeezed his hand goodbye.

He tore his gaze away from the city to look at her. "Thank you! I am forever in your debt," he replied, looking into her sparkling eyes. A part of his mind noticed that they were as dazzling as the crystal spires. Did she feel an unspoken attraction between them, too? Despite their age and cultural differences, he felt oddly comfortable in her presence. Had James not already been happily married, Deleanaa would be exactly the type of girl he'd want to settle down with.

For her part, had she not intended to marry for political advantage, James would have been just the sort of man *she* could have fallen in love with, Deleanaa knew.

They exchanged a knowing glance, and then Deleanaa gave him one last smile and walked down the path into the city, followed by her attendants.

James stayed back behind the line of trees at the edge of the forest. He sat down, leaned against a sturdy tree trunk, and took out a pod manual that had become a sketchbook and journal. Slowly and steadily, he began to draw a picture of the crystal city between pod instructions.

Hours passed; James watched as the sun moved across the sky. He picked wildflowers growing in the shade of the forest's edge and pressed them between the pages of his makeshift journal. Eventually, the sun sank beneath the ocean's blue horizon, a red-and-orange haze melting into the dark blue water. The crystal city glowed in the golden light of the setting sun, the reflective crystal surfaces shimmering like a jewel in the night.

James stepped cautiously onto the long crystal bridge leading into Ectara City. After his earlier experience of crossing the bridge in the forest, he tried his best not to look down as he crossed this bridge. Once or twice curiosity got the best of him, though, and he glanced past his feet despite himself. He saw rough waves turning white as they crashed against rocks hundreds of meters down. The sight made his stomach twist and turn inside his belly.

How can people cross this every day? James wondered. *Perhaps Ectarans have no fear of heights…* Holding his breath, he hurried across the final expanse and into the city proper.

Music filled the air as he entered the city walls, and everywhere he looked, he saw people eating, drinking, and celebrating. At the end of the city, perched on top of a large plateau that fell away to the ocean below, stood a magnificent crystal castle. It appeared to have grown right out of the rocks upon which it was perched. A smaller clear drawbridge connected the city to the castle.

He winced when he saw the drawbridge. Even as a veteran of war and an intergalactic traveler, James felt these bridges were needlessly intimidating. It didn't help that the wind had picked up and a gust nearly blew his tunic right off his shoulder.

He hurried across the bridge and took refuge inside the massive entranceway. The sky was turning darker by the minute, and the light within the castle created a mirror effect in its windows. James turned to look at his reflection and straighten out his tunic.

Inside, the walls of the crystal castle glowed golden with the light they had absorbed during the day, setting a jovial and festive mood. The grand ballroom was a flurry of activity as everyone celebrated the new year. Musicians played a delightful tune; elegantly dressed guests feasted and danced. A long table had been laid out with an assortment of delicacies from the ocean. Various types of seafood dishes that James didn't recognize had obviously been expertly prepared. A dark, sweet wine was being mixed with water and then passed around to the celebrants.

The King and Queen were observing the festivities from their sparkling crystal thrones. James slowly approached them. The music and merriment subsided as he knelt before their thrones, lifting one arm up and grasping his elbow with the other to indicate supplication, a gesture widely adopted throughout the galaxy.

Silence briefly fell on the room; then, a few seconds later, scattered whispers circulated through the hall. From the corner of his eye, James saw Deleanaa standing with other maidens, now dressed in formal attire. She appeared to have transformed from a sweet girl into a regal princess. A faint hint of a smile of encouragement passed over her lips, as if she were saying "Go on, don't give up now."

James bowed his head before addressing the throne. "King and Queen of Ectara, my ship crashed in a meadow across from the forest this afternoon. I am trying to return home to Earth, and I humbly request assistance." His deep voice echoed across the great hall, bouncing off the crystal walls.

There was a long pause as his hosts tried to evaluate the guest and situation. Finally, the King spoke. "Wayward traveler, join us in our festivities. Tonight we celebrate the new year, and we welcome all guests. Afterwards, we will discuss your homecoming." The Queen smiled in agreement and nodded at James as well.

The King gestured to his attendants, and food and wine was offered to James. James bowed once more, then took a sip of wine and a bite of bread.

A singer stepped forward and the musicians resumed playing. The guests listened as the performer told the tale of Hectar in a ballad.

James' universal translator experienced interference from the chemical composition of the crystal palace; due to the malfunction, James was able to hear the Ectaran language in its original and also simultaneously understand its meaning. Listening and understanding the ballad in its original was a little jarring, but also struck him to his core.

"Yi fotar elong.
La key ha delong mar Shatar
Wa hah shatee gar Hectar.
Ha Stellaes sherarie egara
La Stella westara,
Ha sna lenaa squeeskar
Fara ekongarii.
Ha Hectara delongashtar
Vegantar ook sleetala isht.
Puk nan deloti
Arg charneekum wishtar ooteca.
Snagar yine dost, James Odysseus,
Eganatipa shelati wa Earth,
Shala ook skilsa
Ti egamar chaarum whahaala
Ook Sna qua ti foogari wastaar rastii.
Ha Stellaes ook par charier
Ti pleaka puk ha Hectari egakoom.
Latar Cassiel pleekina
Arg ha lenaa chaarum garfelar

Elara arsqua hecataa shtar.
Wapar Cassiel pleekina chia ishti,
Quian arg ark qua sna fikasi sweekar,
Leeka arsqua pentii beentar.
Elarpwi ha chaarum, ti skar nookala.
Lamba ha shtar, ha niimba,
Ha nakala, ha shikala, ook scala
Wa ha Stellaes ishti.
Fleek elarpwi, arg lenaa pri Hectar groandt
Ha stopari char pershi linaar pepii.
Ha shtar leen bit foanti kintook.
Awelt tarp snarp kanti
Qua ha ringata wa facar
Elar ha blita krapeet krapoota toomar.
Dosti, dostari, ook shalwali,
Ecareen toomar.
Stella wetara.
Sarg geenar.

The ballad, James knew, translated to the following:

"Come, O Muses!
Whisper to me the star-crossed tale
of the battle at Hectar.
The Stellaes banded together
to retrieve Stella,
The most beautiful technology
Ever created.
The Hectaran spaceship
Was immense and impenetrable.
For ten years,
They fought with little success.
Until one man, James Odysseus,

Biological engineer of Earth,
Cunning and clever,
Devised a tree horse
And presented it as a parting offering.
The Stellaes packed up and left,
A seeming victory for the Hectarans.
Despite Cassie's warnings,
They took in the beautiful horse,
Taking it into their monstrous ship.
Alas, Cassie's warnings were true!
Though they dismissed her as a lunatic,
That would be their demise.
Inside the horse was concealed a ship;
Onboard the ship were the best,
The brightest, the strongest, and fiercest
Of the Stellaes.
Once inside, they sacked beautiful new Hectar.
The corridors ran red with blood.
The ship fell apart at its seams.
Those who were not taken
As the spoils of war
Perished in the wine-dark space.
Men, women, and children…
All perished.
Stella was retrieved.
None were spared.

A tear welled up in James' eye. Hearing the Ectarans talk about the battle at Hectar and understanding the ballad in its native Ectaran were more than he could take. His emotions started overwhelming him as he remembered and relived those horrible moments, and suddenly he could not contain himself any longer.

He stood, and the singer fell quiet. "*I* am James Odysseus of Earth. *I* am the architect, the engineer of whom you speak." James looked around and saw that all eyes were on him.

He continued. "After ten years of bloody war, we sacked Hectar and took back Stella. I bid my comrades farewell, and we embarked for home. My friend Michael set off for the Asian Union with his ships; his brother Andrew returned to the American Union with his ships. The other Stellaes also departed for their home worlds. Most of us were happy that the war was over." He paused briefly, lost in memories. No one spoke.

"I was eager to return to my wife and son," he finally resumed. "Max had been barely two years old when I had left. I couldn't wait to meet the young man he had become! I thought he'd be thirteen by the time we made it back. I never imagined how everything could go so wrong."

CHAPTER 6

THE JOURNEY

Seven years before James landed on Ectara...

James' five ships—the *Athena, Zelus, Kratos, Nike,* and *Bia*—were flying in formation to Earth. It had been two months since they had left Hectar, and after ten years of war, everyone was more than ready to get home. If everything went according to plan, they would be back on Earth in less than a year.

Each ship had its own captain, and each of the captains reported to James on the *Athena*, a swift and sleek ship. Its bridge was a swarm of activity. Engineering ran diagnostics on the ship's equipment to make sure everything was running at peak efficiency, Communications scanned the void of space for any incoming transmissions, and Navigation double-checked the route set for the journey home.

James sat in the captain's chair, looking over the route on a holographic map of the galaxy. He manipulated the map with his hands, examining the twists and turns from every angle.

"Estimated travel time—accounting for rest and recharging stops—is 237 days and 12 hours," first officer Stewart said as he examined his own charts at his console.

"Everything is going as planned," James cheerfully commented. However, beneath his pleasant disposition, disquiet was brewing in him. Somehow, when everything went a little too well, that made James slightly nervous. He had the oddest predilection that this was all too good to be true. Besides, "according to plan" was also terribly boring.

"When is our next recharging stop?" James asked.

The computer illuminated a point on the map. "Our next recharging stop is in 12 hours and 34 minutes," it told him. "The suggested recharging location is at the following coordinates..." Another bright point appeared.

James swiped away the holographic map and stood up. "Stewart, you have the bridge. I'll be in my quarters. Alert me half an hour prior to our recharging stop."

"Yes, sir," Stewart said as he took the captain's chair. First officer Stewart was as dependable and straightforward as they came—an ideal first officer. He always did things by the book and kept the crew on their toes. James worried at times that Stewart was a bit mechanical; he secretly wondered if Stewart had been replaced with an android. *No, that's ridiculous,* James would always eventually conclude.

James walked off the bridge into his private quarters that were adjacent to the bridge. His room was sparsely decorated, albeit well-illuminated: glow ferns grew out of pots against the walls, simultaneously lighting the bedroom and freshening the air, and a large algae tank hung on one of the walls. Most quarters came with standard-issue small algae tanks that pumped air through the algae for air-quality purposes. However, as captain, James had designed a larger tank for his private quarters that was more akin to an aquarium. He kept a genetically modified sea-sheep pet in it. It was much larger than the typical sea slug, and it mostly spent its time slowly making its way across the tank, eating algae and making room for new algae to grow back. James wasn't sure that the slug had ever noticed or needed him, but still, it felt nice to have someone to "look after." He had nicknamed his pet Homer and checked on his pet daily, watching it chew away meticulously at the algae.

A few halo pictures floated above a shelf in his bookcase. James walked over to them and hovered over an image of Ella and Max. Using his fingers, he enlarged the image until they were almost the same size as him. Every day, James went through this ritual and imagined that his family was right there beside him. If he really concentrated, he could almost hear Ella's beautiful voice. He liked to pretend that she was in the shower or just around the corner and would appear at any second, throw her arms around his neck, and kiss him passionately.

He let the picture go, and the image returned to its regular size on the shelf. It had been ten years since he'd seen his family, and his memories were fading, gradually being replaced with the images and videos he'd seen over and over. Over the past ten years, he had watched all of his homemade holographic videos so many times that he knew every word by heart. His favorite video was the one he had recorded of Ella carrying a birthday cake to Max for his first birthday. He loved to sing along with Ella as she placed the cake in front of little Max, who was grinning from ear to ear, his big chubby baby cheeks so round and plump. Ella looked soft and touchable in the candlelight, her eyes beaming as she watched Max make a wish and blow out the candle.

James had a handful of messages he'd received over the years through the Stellae's transmission system from his family. However, the images were scratchy, and the resolution and sound quality was poor as it had to travel long distances across space to get to him, usually taking over a year to arrive after transmission. He preferred to watch the high-quality videos he had brought with him and remember his family as he had left them.

James blamed his own ambition for getting him into this predicament. Had he not been so eager to expand the company and invest in breakthrough technologies that would change the game for his business, he would not have been contractually obligated to fight a war halfway across the galaxy. He wouldn't have missed all the birthdays, sporting games, family vacations, and lazy Saturday mornings. It was especially those lazy Saturday mornings that he so often wished he could get back. But alas, there was no turning back time.

Sometimes when James was waiting for sleep to overtake him, he imagined he was at home again. He pretended he and Ella were leisurely sleeping in one morning, hoping the sunlight wouldn't wake their toddler son down the hall. What he wouldn't give to roll over and cuddle with his beautiful wife again! James hated the war. The blood, death, and destruction were terrible enough, but the loss of his own personal life and all the magical little moments that could have been was unbearable.

James walked over to his bed and lay down, not even bothering to take off his uniform. What was the point? He was just going to have to put it on again in a few hours. He closed his eyes and let sleep wash over him.

At first, he felt deeply relaxed; then he felt weightless. Soon, time lost its typical rhythm—minutes seemed like hours; hours seemed like seconds. Then dreams faded in and out of his mind. One became another and then turned into a series of disconcerting dreams. At one point, James dreamed he was swimming in the ocean. He was completely alone. There was no land as far as the eye could see. All he had with him was a small makeshift raft made of tree trunks tied together. It was only half-floating above the water. The skies turned dark, and the waves grew as large as mountains.

A giant wave crashed down on James, smashing his tiny raft and pushing him down into the icy water. It was dark and painfully cold under the great expanse of blue. His lungs hurt from the pressure.

With all his might, James swam for the surface. He thought he might run out of breath, but with his last ounce of strength, he managed to barely make it back to the surface. He gasped desperately for air.

Rain started pouring down from the dark sky. It had become night, and the water beneath him was black under the moonless sky. Exhausted and numb with cold, James chose a random point on the horizon and started swimming. *Just keep swimming!* he told himself. When his limbs felt as though they were going to give out and his body felt as though it was sinking into the magnitude of the ocean, he woke up.

Sweat lined his brow. James sat up, disturbed by what he had just experienced. *That felt so real! But it was just a dream...* Still, he couldn't seem to shake the feeling that the dream meant something. In any case, it was soon forgotten, drifting into that mysterious place in the mind where dreams go soon after waking. By the time James stepped back onto the bridge, he had no memory whatsoever of anything he had dreamed the night before.

Days turned into weeks, and the steady rhythm of daily routines took over. Boredom set in. The same patterns of warp, rest, recharge, warp, rest, recharge, repeated over and over. James would later be ashamed to admit it, but secretly, he wished for adventure—anything to break up the monotony of the long voyage home.

For sixty days, their return trip home went just as planned, with one day indistinguishable from the next. The crew became comfortable. They performed their duties as usual, although they were no longer actively looking for abnormalities. They didn't have any sense of urgency. The war had been won, and their contracts were almost over. Everyone would return home and take a much-deserved vacation.

Day 61 began just like any other day. As usual, an alarm went off in James' quarters at 6 AM Coordinated Universal Time. James woke up, splashed water on his face, left his quarters, and went for a jog around the ship. He had long ago given up eating breakfast—instead, he tried to get a little exercise in the morning before starting his day. This time, though, he saw a young cadet eating a donut on his third lap around the ship, and for some reason, that made him extraordinarily hungry.

Rather than finishing his workout, he headed right for the mess hall and helped himself to scrambled eggs, toast, and fruit. He had never really liked space food—he vastly preferred food cooked and grown the old-fashioned way. Food assembled on the spot atom-by-atom had never entirely agreed with him, but seeing as he had been traveling for years on end through space, his options had been rather limited for quite some time.

Back on the bridge, it was business as usual, with the crew on duty running their standard diagnostic reviews and scans. James took his seat in the captain's chair. He did a secondary review of the ship's diagnostic reports, examined the route home, and checked in with Engineering and Navigation. James liked his crew and found them to be a mostly agreeable lot, but he knew they were all a tad lazy, too. They needed to be reminded of the seriousness of their duties every once in a while—otherwise, operations would fall behind.

First officer Stewart gave his report. "Sir, we've maintained warp for the past 12 hours. We are preparing to stop to recharge and run a diagnostic on the core. Also, Engineering reports that *Zelus* has almost depleted their supply of Zypherus crystals."

James considered alternative actions. "Can we redirect crystals from one of the other ships?" he asked.

Stewart replied, "Perhaps for a few days, sir. However, we'll need to acquire more within a week. All of our ships' Zypherus crystal supplies are beginning to run low."

"Map," James said. A large holographic map of the Milky Way appeared in the middle of the bridge. The stars twinkled in a beautiful formation, letting the crew on the deck see the cosmos from a privileged perspective, as though they were gods looking down on the galaxy from afar.

James started to examine the star map. A blinking point of light indicated their position. "Chart current route," he instructed. A white line appeared charting their route thus far; a blue line showed the rest of the intended route to Earth.

"Pallas, list all refueling ports along our current route that have trading hubs known to deal in Zephyrus crystals." A few red points popped up on the map. James zoomed in, manipulating the map with his hands. He zoomed in even closer and examined a few planets. The first planet looked red and barren, so he chose another. That planet looked mostly yellow and gray. He zoomed out again and honed in on a third planet. The third planet looked blue and green, similar to Earth.

James double-tapped a finger on its image. "Pallas, what do we know about this planet?" he asked, taking a step back.

"Planet Decta has a peaceful merchant culture and is similar to Earth in its topography," the computer promptly stated. "Decta is known for its vibrant forest marketplace and their renowned decta fruit, often consumed in a tropical cocktail concoction."

Glancing around the bridge, James noticed that the cadets seemed excited and enthusiastic about the idea of going to Decta. Even first officer Stewart—who was usually the naysayer—seemed to think it was a good option. "Set a course for Decta," James commanded, then turned to the communications officer. "Francis, notify all ships of our new plans."

"Yes, sir," Francis said as he prepped a message for the other ships.

A few hours later, the ships came out of warp in sight of the blue-green planet. It swirled like an aquamarine jewel in the darkness of space, with one side illuminated by the sun and the other resting in shadow. Three moons circled the planet.

"Engineering, initiate solar recharging," James ordered. "And while we're here, also run a full diagnostic on the core."

"Yes, sir," engineering officer Thomas responded.

"Stewart, put together a small landing crew," James said before standing up.

"Copy that," Stewart replied.

"Drew, you have the bridge," James said as he headed for the corridor.

"Yes, sir." Second officer Drew moved towards the captain's chair.

Stewart tapped a few cadets on the shoulder, choosing Eli, Rumi, José, and Ken. They assigned their own replacements at their stations, then followed Stewart down a long corridor and into a cargo bay. They quickly and efficiently outfitted a small shuttle with supplies and containers to hold anything they might want to bring back from the planet.

James was already aboard the shuttle. He could barely contain his excitement. This would be his first time on solid ground in eleven years! He couldn't wait to feel real gravity again, let his feet sink into the ground, and breathe fresh air. "What took you ladies so long?" he grumbled as they boarded and buckled up.

The hatch to the shuttle closed and James powered up the engine. The doors to the cargo bay opened, revealing a rectangular patch of space. The men held their breath in anticipation as the shuttle zoomed out and made its way to Decta.

CHAPTER 7:

PLANET DECTA

The shuttle sliced through the planet's atmosphere, soaring over mountains, lush tropical forests, and turquoise waters. The jungles were thick with unusual alien species of vegetation. Seas of dark green and purple leaves tumbled over one another, vibrant flora and fauna fighting for dominance in the densely vegetated landscape.

The shuttle landed on a stretch of pristine beach. The sand sparkled the color of fool's gold and extended for several kilometers along the coast. At the edge of the beach, the plant life came right up to the sand line. James took some pictures with his tablet, excited to learn more about the exotic flora and fauna. He couldn't wait to get some samples to study back in the lab. *What kind of new biological engineering and design breakthroughs might come out of researching these plants?* he wondered. At his heart, James was a creative man, a storyteller, and a biological architect. He was happiest in his lab—amidst his research, he could get lost in thought and lose track of time.

As he scanned the landscape, James noticed a creek meandering out of a break in the jungle and bleeding into the ocean. Stewart, who had been studying his maps on his tablet, looked up. "Sir, the marketplace is that way," he said, pointing towards the creek.

"Great! Looks like we have our path laid out for us!" James joked. His happiness at being back on solid ground was making him uncharacteristically chipper. Space had never agreed with him—solid ground was so much better. And the chance for a little adventure didn't sound so bad, either.

"Ken, guard the ship. The rest of you are with us." James slapped Stewart on the back and then led the men towards the jungle.

They followed the creek towards the direction of the marketplace. James was 41, but he liked to think of himself as a young and athletic man, and he took pride in leading the young cadets as they pushed aside thick foliage and climbed up the steep terrain. *Not over the hill yet*, he thought to himself, noticing that José was sweating profusely and Eli was holding his side and out of breath.

"Hey, lads, you need me to hire you a Sherpa?" James chuckled.

"The market is just another kilometer northwest, sir," Stewart stated. His eyes were on his tablet as he said that; seconds later, he inadvertently walked right into a prickly bush.

The sweaty cadets could hardly contain their laughter. James pretended not to notice. Although Steward was an extremely organized first officer, it amazed James how physically uncoordinated he could be at times.

As they made their way through the jungle, James paused from time to time to pluck a leaf or clip a vine. He tucked the samples away in small vials and stowed them in his sack. As he was tucking a particularly interesting purple reed into a vial, he heard a rustling in the bush. He held up a hand to indicate a stop.

They all paused and listened, but the rustling stopped, too. The men continued on. A few steps further along the path, they heard it again.

"Pallas, are there any dangerous species in this jungle?" Stewart asked his tablet.

"Affirmative," the computer replied. "Two species dangerous to humanoid life forms are native to the Dectan jungle." An image of a venomous arachnid appeared on the tablet next to an image of a large feline-like creature with green scales and jagged, interlocking teeth.

The crew looked at the images of the monstrous creatures and stood still, hardly breathing, listening carefully for any sounds that might indicate that a vicious predator was present in the jungle.

José looked up to see if any creepy insects were descending on them—he was unusually afraid of spiders. When he had been a young boy playing in the garden outside his childhood home, he had felt a tickling sensation on the back of his right arm. He had thought it was the tall grass and ignored it, but when the tickling sensation persisted, he had finally twisted his head over his shoulder to examine the back of his arm...and was disgusted to see a large spider attached to it and about to bite him. He had immediately swatted it away, but it was too late. Soon after, a large cyst the size of a quail egg had formed under the skin.

At the doctor's office, they told him they had to remove the cyst and gave him an anesthetic. For some reason, it didn't work, and patients in the hallway later said they could hear his murderous screams as the doctors sliced the cyst out of his arm. He had been terrified of spiders ever since.

A small fly-like bug landed on José's shoulder. He spun around, batting it away and making a lot of noise in the process. The other men looked at him, half-annoyed, half-scared that he might have drawn the attention of a real predator towards them.

Suddenly, there was a louder rustling noise in the bushes, as if an animal were moving with great speed through the foliage. The men drew their weapons and held their breath, half-expecting to see a giant scaled cat pounce on them from behind the bushes. Instead, a spotted purple-feathered gazelle-like creature dashed past them. Relieved and amused, they pressed on.

As they continued to follow the stream up a steep incline, their quadriceps and calves started to burn. The gravity on the planet felt heavier since Decta was nearly twice the mass of Earth, and the increased pull made the men get slightly out of breath. James didn't mind, though—he was happy for the exercise, fresh air, and promise of adventure. His crew, however, were far less enthusiastic. Eli kept imagining that lasers were shooting out of his eyes into Stewart's back for selecting him for this mission.

Just when they were ready to take a break, the brush opened up, revealing a teeming marketplace. It had been built into both sides of a dramatic canyon that plunged thousands of meters down into the forest. Clearly, a river had run over the soft stone for thousands of years and had cut away at the terrain, creating a stunningly beautiful landscape of terraced stone and cascading waters. Lush vegetation filled in every crevice available, and colorful winged insects, feathered animals, and other unusual creatures fluttered around in the open spaces.

James noticed a squirrel-like creature with large multicolored wings sitting on a branch and eating what looked like berries. Then he saw an arachnid-like insect with a tail reminiscent of a scorpion immobilize a small bird with something that shot out of its tail. It proceeded to wrap up its prey in grey silk. *How intriguing*, he thought, simultaneously glad he was too big to be wrapped in silk.

James took a deep breath and soaked in all the newness of their surroundings. He wished he had more time to categorize the flora and fauna. This was exactly the kind of adventure he had been hankering for to break up the monotony of space travel!

Several waterfalls cascaded down through the middle of the marketplace, ending in the creek that the crew had followed from the shore.

Stewart indicated the cliff where vendors had built their shops into the side of the canyon. "The crystal trader is over this way," he said.

"Come to papa," James muttered under his breath.

"What was that?" Stewart asked.

"Oh nothing," James replied with a quick shake of his head.

Stewart found James' behavior annoyingly erratic at times. He felt that a good leader should embody stability, logic, and predictability—cadets, he felt, should be able to predict what kind of response their actions would elicit from their commanding officers. He felt that James' inconsistency would lead to disobedience and laziness if left unchecked. Stewart also felt that it was his duty to keep the crew in line while faithfully executing the captain's orders to the best of his ability, so he did his best to mute any critical thoughts that came to mind.

James examined the steep and narrow path leading to the vendors, then looked at his clumsy and out-of-breath men. "No point in us all going up there," James said, worried that one might fall off the cliff or hinder the trade. He decided to offer them an out. "Scout the marketplace for other potential crystal vendors—we might need a backup if the first seller tries to gouge us. Also, keep an eye out for anything suspicious. Marketplaces in this section of the galaxy are known for having pickpockets and swindlers." He looked at each of them in turn. "And one more thing: be ready to head back to the ship the moment we return."

"Yes, sir," they all replied in unison. James nodded once, and he and Stewart strode away from the rest of the crew.

When James and Stewart were out of view, Eli, Rumi, and José relaxed a little.

"Come on, guys, you heard the captain. Let's go have a little fun!" Eli said, throwing his arm around Rumi and walking down the path to the lower-level vendors.

"That's not what the captain said at all!" José butted in.

"Oh, lighten up!" Rumi told him. "Life is short—you gotta find fun while you're still kicking."

José just shook his head and followed his friends, hoping they wouldn't get into too much trouble.

The three of them explored the lower marketplace, observing various stalls and the merchants' wares.

"Fried bugs! Get your delicious fried bugs!" a vendor shouted. They kept walking.

An old lady came out and grabbed Eli by the wrist. "Nice watches," she said, holding up an array of timepieces. "For you, very good price!"

"No, thanks," Eli replied, wiggling free from her grasp.

A young woman with an innocent face stepped forward holding a large fruit that resembled a purple coconut. It had a velvety flower on top. The girl tilted her head, indicating that the men should follow her into her shop. Eli and Rumi started to follow, but José objected. "Guys, I don't think this is a good idea. We should keep scouting for crystal vendors. Remember what the captain said!"

"A little fun's not going to kill us," Rumi replied. José shrugged and reluctantly followed them into the shop.

Meanwhile, James and Stewart climbed up the narrow, harrowing steps along the side of the canyon, passing dozens of tiny little shops cut right into the side of the cliff. Stewart glanced at his tablet. "Over here—this is it," he said.

They stopped in front of a medium-sized shop with a sign that said "Crystals, Gems, and Unusual Galactic Metals. Intergalactic B+ rating." They peeked inside the shop's few windows, then went through the small door and squeezed themselves into the tiny crystal shop.

Shelves were stacked with countless rows of jars and clear boxes of various assortments of crystals, gems, and metals collected from across the galaxy. The ceiling was low, and James and Stewart had to stoop a little so as not to hit their heads. Still, Stewart forgot his height and bumped his head a few times. The compact space, low ceiling, and tightly packed inventory all added to a feeling of claustrophobia.

"May I help you?" a small, wrinkled man asked from behind the counter. He had long, pointed, gray-brown ears. Several folds of skin served as eyebrows above his small and squinty eyes. His skin was mostly grayish-blue in color, and he wore a burgundy cloak made of an obviously expensive and finely woven fabric.

"Yes, I believe you can. We're in the market for some crystals," James said with the friendliest demeanor possible.

"Then you've come to the right place!" the vendor replied.

"We're looking for Zypherus crystals," Stewart said bluntly.

The vendor raised a fleshy eyebrow. "Well, now, those are hard to come by. But you're in luck—I have some! Not many crystal vendors carry them seeing as they are in short supply these days. One moment, please."

The vendor pulled a sliding ladder towards himself, climbed up to the ceiling, moved aside a ceiling panel, and continued up into an attic space. Moments later, he came back down the ladder with a box in his hands. He turned to James and Stewart and placed the box on the counter. Carefully, he removed the lid, revealing a clear container. Inside were blue crystals that sparkled in the store's bright lights.

"May I?" Stewart asked.

"Of course," the merchant replied.

Stewart opened the container and used the merchant's wooden tongs to pick up one of the blue crystals. It wasn't more than 10 centimeters in diameter. He pulled out his tablet and scanned the crystal. When he zoomed in, the tablet authenticated its compounds. "This will do," Stewart said, placing the crystal back carefully in the container.

"How much?" James asked.

"How many do you need?" was the merchant's reply.

"Five units," Stewart specified.

The merchant input some numbers into a tablet and handed it over to the men.

James raised an eyebrow. "Half," he said, pushing back the tablet.

The vendor looked irate. "That's below my cost. I'm sorry... Maybe I can lower the price by ten percent, but that's all I can do." At this point in the negotiations, the merchant knew that most foreign buyers would accept a ten-percent discount.

James, however, was not most foreign buyers. He had traveled extensively throughout the galaxy, and he took pride in getting the best prices and most value for his currency. He knew there was an art to bargaining—it was one part market statistics and one part bluffing. He looked the merchant over, trying to guess his rock-bottom price. "Half," James said, sticking to his initial offer. "Take it or leave it."

The merchant shook his head and packed up the box.

James nudged Stewart, and they headed for the door. The vendor nervously watched them out of the corner of his eye. The two men left the shop and started making their way back to the steep stairs.

Stewart made sure they were out of earshot, then grabbed James by the arm and barked in a loud whisper, "What the hell are you doing?"

James removed Stewart's hand from his arm. "Haven't you ever heard of a little thing called bargaining? It's a common practice in these parts."

"Need I remind you that we desperately need those crystals?" Stewart nearly spat out. "Who knows if there is another seller for light years around here? This is no time to be frugal. Suck it up and pay whatever he's asking!"

"Relax!" James reassured him. "Just keep walking."

Stewart looked mutinous, but he obeyed; they continued walking away at a leisurely pace. James held up his fingers and counted aloud: "In 3, 2, 1..."

On the mark, the vendor came running out of the shop with a small box in his hands. "Fine, fine, take it! Deal." He acted annoyed as he threw the box at them.

Stewart caught the box, shocked by the merchant's sudden change of heart and also relieved he hadn't dropped the precious merchandise.

James opened his tablet and pressed a few buttons. "Transferring funds now. It was a pleasure doing business with you." James smiled as he took the box from Stewart and put it into his sack.

Back at the rendezvous point, the cadets were nowhere to be found. James and Stewart scoured the marketplace for the missing cadets as inconspicuously as they could, quietly poking their heads into stalls and searching for their men without drawing unnecessary attention to themselves.

After a few minutes, James peeked through an open doorway and caught a glimpse of one of the cadets dancing in a bar. He did a double-take. "Over here! Found 'em," James said, half-angry and half-amused. They reminded him a little of his younger self, before life and its responsibilities had tamed him. He had half a mind to let them have their fun.

When the cadets had first entered the bar, the barkeep girl had brought over an entire tray of the flowering fruits she had initially showed them. Eli leaned in to smell the local delicacies, taking in a deep whiff of their subtle aroma. "Enchanting…" he said, looking the girl up and down.

José grumbled, "Keep it in your pants, cadet!"

"Lighten up, José," Eli retorted. "I'm just having a little fun. You should try it sometime."

The girl smiled, pulling out a sharp metal straw from her apron. With swift dexterity, she plunged the straw into the fruit, then handed it to Eli. "Dec-ta," she enunciated slowly.

The young cadet grasped the exotic drink with both hands and took a long, satisfying sip from the straw. His eyes closed as he savored the experience. "Guys, you have to try this! It's amazing." Eli said. He headed for the plush couches against the wall, still clutching his drink. The girl handed drinks to José and Rumi, and they reluctantly followed Eli.

Minutes later, the hallucinogenic properties of the drink had taken effect: Eli reclined on a cushioned bench, José was half-sprawled over the bar, and Rumi danced alone in the middle of the room even though no music was playing.

José shouted, "Drinks for everyone!" No one seemed to notice—they were all absorbed in their own hallucinations. Eli stared at his hands, convinced his skin was moving. Jose was having a very animated conversation with himself, thinking that Ruben—his best friend from his childhood—had just shown up at the bar. Rumi seemed to think there was a crazy party going on as he pointed and winked at an imaginary girl he thought he was flirting with him across the bar.

The barkeep had seen it all before and was unfazed. She offered the men another round of drinks. Eli took one, slurped deeply, then fell asleep, still holding the drink.

That was when James and Stewart walked in. "Party's over! Time to head back," James said, clapping his hands loudly. No one noticed.

Stewart made an attempt, raising his voice to get their attention. "Attention, cadets, your captain is speaking to you!" Still no one noticed.

James went over to Eli, who was slumped over on the cushioned bench, unconscious. His head was resting on a silk cushion embroidered with images of decta fruits, and although his eyes were closed, his eyelids were rapidly moving back and forth.

James shook Eli, but he didn't wake up—instead, he mumbled something incomprehensible and rolled over, falling off the bench and onto the floor.

"What the hell has gotten into you?" James asked, looking around at his men.

The girl came around with a tray of drinks. Rumi lunged for the tray, barely able to grab one of the drinks. James instinctively slapped it out of his hand. It went crashing to the floor, and in seconds, a pale white fluid had collected into a puddle on the ground.

Without even hesitating, Rumi was on his hands and knees like a dog, lapping up the liquid off the filthy floor.

"Looks like now we know what's gotten into them," Stewart said, eyeing the drinks.

James sighed and shook his head. "We're going to have to carry them back."

James and Stewart grabbed Rumi by either arm and dragged him out of the bar. When he realized what they were doing, Rumi started to resist. He clawed at them and screamed, "Let me stay! Leave me here! I want to stay!"

Eventually, Stewart had to hold him down while James injected him with a sedative. They carried Eli back to the ship and then repeated the arduous process with the other cadets. Due to the steep incline of the path and the stronger gravitational pull of the planet, by the time they brought the third cadet back to the shuttle, James and Stewart were out of breath, exhausted, and sore.

"I'd fire them all if we were back on Earth," James grumbled to Stewart.

"Lord knows you've done worse in your younger days," Stewart reminded him.

The sun was setting over the water as they loaded the still-unconscious cadets onto the shuttle. James stopped for a moment to take in the beauty of the red and gold light of the setting sun rippling across the waves of the dark sea. He grabbed a fistful of sand and put it into his pocket before boarding the shuttle.

CHAPTER 8

CYCLOPS

Not soon after the shuttle had landed in Cargo Bay 2 back onboard *Athena*, James, Stewart, and Ken stepped out of the hatch, covered in dried sweat and mud and carrying the box of crystals. Eli, Rumi, and José were still out cold.

"Captain to Sickbay," James said. "I need a team of medics to report to Cargo Bay 2. We have three cadets requiring medical attention."

"Sickbay here," chief medic Daniel responded promptly. "On our way, sir."

Ken stayed behind to debrief the medical team about what had happened with the cadets on Decta while James and Stewart made their way to the bridge. Although James had originally been excited about being on solid ground again, after what had transpired, he felt that he had finally learned the meaning of the phrase "too much of a good thing" and was more than happy to be back onboard his ship. Stewart, he noticed, looked like he felt the same way. James had the feeling that Stewart looked disdainfully upon disorder, and this past excursion had certainly seemed to rub him the wrong way.

When the bridge doors slid open, James was pleased to see that everything was just as he had left it. He handed the crystals to

Thomas, telling him, "Get that down to Engineering right away. And tell Engineering to send provisions to the other ships ASAP."

"Yes, sir," Thomas replied. He quickly left the bridge.

"Status report," James said.

Second officer Drew reported, "Recharging completed. Solar batteries at 100%. Standard mechanical and electrical checks completed."

"Excellent," James said, relieved that at least things had gone as planned in his absence. Whenever he stepped away from his ship, his biggest worry was that something would go wrong and that he might have been able to prevent unnecessary disaster if he hadn't left the ship. Although his crew was well-trained and experienced, when push came to shove, James felt he had better intuition and common sense than the lot of them.

"Resume course for Earth," James commanded, sitting down in the captain's chair. He hated to admit it, but he felt rather satiated by the bit of adventure he had had on Decta. *Although I could have certainly done without the latter half of the day*, he thought.

"Aye, sir," said Jin, the navigation officer. Jin double-checked the plotted course and executed the sequence on the navigation console.

"Course resumed. Prepare to warp in 10, 9, 8, 7, 6, 5, 4, 3, 2, 1..." the computer said.

The crew braced themselves as the ship jumped into warp. After a few minutes, the officers and cadets relaxed. "I presume the mission was a success?" Drew asked.

James and Stewart exchanged a knowing look and tried to suppress the urge to laugh. "We got what we were looking for, yes. But not everything went exactly as planned," James admitted.

Stewart elaborated, "Some of the cadets encountered an exotic fruit drink that appears to have psychedelic properties."

James had to tell his crew the truth. "They didn't remember who the hell they were or what we were doing there, and we had to knock them out and drag them back to the shuttle." He burst into laughter.

Stewart stopped trying to contain himself and cracked up as well. The rest of the deck seemed slightly amused, but not as amused as James and Stewart.

James got up. "I'll be in my quarters. Stewart, you should wash up—your uniform is filthy. Drew, you have the bridge." Stewart nodded and left the bridge a half-second before James did.

James entered his quarters, prompting the glow-light plants to turn on. He undressed and threw his soiled uniform into a washing machine/dryer box on the wall. "Clean uniform," James said. The compartment locked, a light switched on, and enhanced plant enzymes mixed with water began trickling over his garments.

James stepped into the shower and let hot water run over his face. Once his curly hair got wet, it lengthened and fell into his eyes, so he closed them.

Memories streamed unbidden through his mind. James remembered rolling around under crisp white sheets, making love with his beautiful wife in the early hours of the morning as the first rays of sun streaked across the sky. Her soft, sweet voice echoed through his mind. James loved the sound of her laughter; he clung to the memory of her giggling. He retraced the feeling of running his hands down her sides, recalling the warmth of her soft thighs pressed into his. He remembered slowly tracing the line of her neck as it turned into her clavicle, formed a ridge across her collarbone, and curved into her shoulder. With a tugging feeling of yearning, James remembered how much he loved the scent of her skin as he kissed her shoulder.

Sighing, he turned off the water and stepped out of the shower. A blast of warm air dried him in a matter of seconds and brusquely brought him back into the present. He grabbed his clean and dry uniform out of the compartment on the wall. The material was warm to the touch as he pulled it on. *One of the few pleasures in space is clean, warm uniforms right out of the box*, he thought gratefully.

He sat down on the edge of his bed and glanced over at the holographic pictures of his family on the shelf, thinking of one of the last conversations he'd had with Ella. He winced as he remembered how he had yelled at her. Now he couldn't even remember what the argument had been about… His chest felt heavy, and he wished he could take back his unkind words. Sometimes he got so hot-headed, he knew, that angry words fell out of his mouth, things he'd later wish he could take back.

"Pallas, play the video of Max's second birthday," he said aloud. A video appeared of two-year-old Max sitting at a table, wearing a red party hat, and holding a bioluminescent flower that glowed bright purple. Max grinned a giant gummy smile, flashing his tiny baby teeth. Ella walked into view carrying a vanilla layered cake topped with rainbow sprinkles and candles. James thought she looked particularly beautiful in the candlelight.

Guests were singing "Happy Birthday" in the background. "Happy Birthday, Max," Ella said. "Make a wish and blow out the candles!"

James mouthed the words as she said them. He had watched every video in his library countless times. Sometimes re-watching the videos made him feel closer to his loved ones, but sometimes it made him feel even more distant when he thought about how much they had changed since he had last seen them. Apart from a few brief, scratchy, messages, he'd received while away, he had no idea who they'd become. Exhausted, James closed his eyes, waiting for sleep to overtake him.

He had the dream again that he was lost at sea. This time, the large waves were as tall as mountains. One came crashing down with the full force of its weight, pummeling into his makeshift raft. He found himself so deep under the cold, dark waves that as hard as he tried to swim to the surface, he couldn't quite reach the top. His ears were pounding with the pressure.

A loud noise suddenly woke James. He opened his eyes and realized he was hearing the sound of the emergency alarm system. Still feeling half-asleep, James darted out of his quarters and onto the bridge. Red emergency lights were flashing along the floors; the crew was struggling to complete their duties amidst the turbulence. The ship shifted suddenly, and a cadet got knocked off his feet and hit his head on his console.

On the screen was an image of a robotic creature that resembled a giant metal insect, with four legs, two tentacle-like arms, mandibles, and a long, curving tail. It was following the ships in close pursuit.

"What the hell is that??" James said in shock, staring at the screen.

"Sir, it appears to be an AI creature, and our scans indicate that it is highly intelligent," First Officer Stewart answered.

"Any notable characteristics?" James asked.

"Affirmative. It appears to have one central sensor that's picking up audio, visual, x-rays, ultraviolet… We're calling it 'Cyclops,' sir."

"What does it want?" James asked.

"It's unclear, but it is trying to attack us," Stewart replied.

"Yeah, I got that much," James said. "Francis, open a channel to all ships."

"Yes, sir. Audio is live to all ships," replied Francis.

James pressed a few buttons on his chair's console. "This is Captain James Odysseus. We are under attack by what appears to be an AI creature. All ships are to immediately drop out of warp at the following coordinates and proceed with evasive maneuvers. Fire at will."

"Ending warp in 10, 9, 8, 7, 6, 5, 4, 3, 2, 1…" the computer said just before they jumped out of warp.

All five ships—the *Athena, Nike, Zelus, Kratos,* and *Bia*—jumped out of warp. The Cyclops appeared a few seconds behind them. On the screen, several ships in close proximity moved apart, spun, and swerved. *Zelus* fired at the creature, hitting it on the side of its body. The Cyclops took notice but appeared unharmed.

It turned its attention to the ship that had fired. The Cyclops moved in with surprising speed, grabbed the ship with two tentacle arms, disintegrated it with its laser mandibles, and consumed the entire ship and the energy caused by its combustion through a mechanical feeder. The crew onboard the *Athena* stared slack jawed in disbelief.

They had already traveled halfway across the galaxy and survived a bloody war. Yet until this moment, it had never occurred to James that he might lose an entire ship in a matter of seconds. He looked around the bridge, his ears ringing. It seemed as though time had slowed down momentarily.

The four remaining ships continued their evasive maneuvers while firing at the Cyclops. The sounds of battle and lasers firing spurred James back into action. "Pallas, generate a hologram of the AI creature," he instructed.

A holographic replica of the creature appeared in the center of the bridge. James examined it from every angle, trying to focus despite a distracting pounding in his ears. He could feel his blood pressure rising. "All ships, fire at will! Lasers, torpedoes, hit it with everything we've got!" he shouted.

Athena hung back to observe the situation, and *Bia* and *Kratos* flanked the Cyclops, firing repeatedly as they moved past it. The AI life form appeared to be annoyed but unharmed. It lunged for *Bia*, captured the ship in its mandibles, and consumed it in one swift motion.

James broke into a sweat. He had lost two of his five ships in a matter of minutes! Calculating the number of lives lost made him feel weak in the knees. He staggered a little and leaned on a console to catch his balance. His vision went blurry for a moment. Rubbing his eyes let him see clearly again, but the momentary blurriness had given him an idea.

"James to *Nike* and *Kratos*. Target the creature's central sensory component. If we can knock out its sensors, it will be flying blind," he said firmly.

"Copy that!" the commanders on the other ships shouted back in unison.

Nike and *Kratos* darted in and out of proximity to the Cyclops, firing repeatedly on its central sensory component. After several passes, they had hardly made a dent. However, the creature seemed increasingly annoyed. Electric sparks ricocheted off its ruffled metal surfaces as it zig-zagged and tried to protect its central sensory component with two of its tentacle-like legs.

James examined the holographic replica of the Cyclops again, zooming in on its central sensory component. It appeared to be heavily fortified and reinforced.

"We need something stronger. Thomas, what if we ejected our core and imploded it on the Cyclops?"

In the midst of the chaos, Thomas looked thoughtful. "It might create an explosion large enough to do the trick," he answered after a brief pause. "It's risky—we'd need to get closer. Also, it would leave us stranded without warp capabilities."

"Sir, I recommend we warp out of here and attempt to outrun this thing," Stewart suggested.

James shook his head adamantly. "It found us in warp and outran us before—it will do it again."

Stewart shook his head. "That could have been an accident, sir. It is highly improbable that a creature could track a ship moving at warp speed."

James paused to consider his first officer's suggestion. Stewart had a point, but something in James' gut told him they had to stand and fight, and his instincts had served him well so far. "Noted. Bring

Nike closer to lure in the creature as we prep our core. When I give the order, move *Nike* aside, then get us in as close as possible and eject the core into its central sensory center," he commanded. Stewart nodded stiffly.

Nike swooped in closer to the Cyclops, firing lasers to get its attention. The other two ships moved in formation behind. The Cyclops lunged at *Nike*. As it did, *Athena* darted around the other ship and got closer to the Cyclops, sliding in dangerously close to the "eye." *Athena* swiftly ejected its core.

It imploded upon contact. The force of the explosion pushed the three ships clear. The "eye" was clearly destroyed—in its place was a gaping hole right in the center of the creature. Bits of metal debris floated outwards, scattering around the three ships as the crews all cheered wildly. The Cyclops retreated into the darkness of space.

The *Athena's* bridge was damaged, James saw as he looked around. Smoke was coming out of some of the consoles; one of the cadets was putting out small fires with a handheld flame retardant device.

"Report," James said hesitantly, not really wanting to hear the news.

"The ship is badly damaged," second officer Drew reported. "On top of that, without our core, we're stranded here. Thrusters work, but we can't warp."

James looked around at the bridge. At least a medical team had arrived. One medic was handing first officer Stewart gauze and telling him to apply pressure to the side of his head that was bleeding. "Casualties?" James asked through his teeth.

"A report is being assembled now, sir," Drew responded. After a brief pause, he said, "*Zelus* and *Bia* were destroyed, of course. There were 362 crew onboard those ships. Aboard our ship, so far we have three reported dead and 15 injured."

James paced the length of the deck, deliberating as to how to proceed. "Prepare to abandon ship," he finally said. "Split the crew and reassign them to the two remaining ships. Pack up all useful supplies, provisions, and equipment. All injured will be transferred to the Sickbay onboard their newly assigned ship." He spoke with a heavy heart.

Meanwhile, in the darkness of space, the wounded Cyclops sputtered along, moving slowly in the void. It was sending out a distress call on a low-wave frequency used by its kind.

Far off in the distance, the creature's kin recognized the call for help and rushed to its aid. A herd of mechanical creatures surrounded the wounded Cyclops to try to repair and mend it. To an untrained ear, the low-wave frequency they used to communicate sounded like the grating of metal.

The wounded Cyclops told its herd about the "evil spaceships" that had "blinded it." The other AI creatures were outraged and vowed to seek vengeance. A band of them set off to hunt down and annihilate the remaining ships.

James took his place on the bridge of the *Nike*, relieving the commanding officer. "All crew is present and accounted for," Stewart told him after he had taken his own position. "Although the situation is slightly cramped, the crewmembers can double up in their quarters." The wound on his temple seemed to have stopped bleeding.

"Are you sure you feel good enough to be on the bridge?" James asked him. "Do you want to rest in Sickbay?"

"At a time like this, I couldn't rest in Sickbay, sir. I'm functional. I've been cleared by the medical team and would prefer to be of service," Stewart replied.

"Very well. Even with half a functioning brain, there'd be no one more qualified for the job," James said with a small smile. "Resume course for Earth."

"And the *Athena*?" Stewart asked.

"Leave it," James replied.

Thomas was at the engineering console, double-checking that all systems were a go. He looked up. "Systems ready, sir."

Eli tapped a few buttons on his navigation panel. "Course set for Earth. Ready to resume on your mark."

"Pallas, engage protocols for warp," James stated.

"Initiating warp in 10, 9, 8, 7, 6, 5, 4, 3, 2, 1..."

The crew braced themselves. *Nike* and *Kratos* jumped into warp, leaving behind the stranded ship. *Athena* sat all alone, abandoned to the emptiness of space, a tiny speck in the immense black void.

After a few moments in warp, the crew relaxed and began their diagnostics. James resumed pacing around the deck. "I want everyone on high alert," he announced. "Notify me if anything seems even slightly suspicious. I'm going to check in on the wounded—I'll be in Sickbay." He nodded to Stewart and walked off the bridge.

James walked down a connecting corridor and around a bend. He'd spent ten years on these ships and knew them inside and out. While the carnage he had experienced at Hectar had been terrible, it was nothing compared to the shock he was currently experiencing. *I lost three ships and hundreds of crewmembers in a matter of hours!*

James blamed himself for wishing for adventure. Slow, steady, and boring would seem like a godsend at this point. Suddenly out of breath and unable to move, James stopped at a window and peered out at space, watching the stars stream by in elongated lines of light.

He leaned against the wall, tears welling up in his eyes. *Pull yourself together!* he told himself. *Not for you, but for the crew! They need a strong leader to get through this.* Besides, he had not yet given up on the hope of being reunited with his family. *I've got to get home!*

James thought. *I've got to get home to Ella and Max.* He wiped the tears off his face and kept walking.

When he entered Sickbay, he saw medics attending to wounded crewmembers lying on medical beds. James approached each one and spoke with them individually. He noticed José in the corner and went over to him. "How are you feeling, cadet?" James asked.

"I've been better," José admitted. A large shard of shrapnel was sticking out of his thigh. "The doc said he'll get to me as soon as he can," he said, eyeing the more pressing cases. One man had suffered third-degree burns on his face, hands, and arms; another had a broken rib sticking out of his uniform.

"Hang in there, soldier," James said before moving on to the next injured patient.

Unbeknownst to the crew onboard *Nike* and *Kratos*, the band of Cyclops had tracked the ships and was getting closer by the minute. The AI creatures had traced the ships' warp signature and used advanced computing programs to target their trajectory, allowing them to jump into warp along the same path and eventually catch up. The Cyclops were quickly gaining on the ships.

By the time the crew on the bridge had detected the creatures, it was too late. "Sir, I can't believe it, but there's an AI creature tailing us, and it's not alone," Francis reported, his voice trembling.

"Put it on the screen," Stewart ordered.

When Francis did, the crew saw a gang of Cyclops in close proximity. One of the larger ones lunged for *Kratos*. Everyone on the bridge stared in disbelief as they watched the AI creature catch *Kratos* between its mandibles. With one fell swoop, it destroyed and consumed the ship.

A momentary hush fell over the deck. Although it only lasted a fraction of a second, it felt like an eternity of silent shock and horror as the crew realized *Nike* was now the only surviving ship.

Half a second later, Stewart regained his senses and sprang into action. "Get us out of warp immediately!" Stewart shouted.

"Yes, sir!" Eli responded. *Nike* jumped out of warp, and the ship came to a bumpy halt in a rarely traveled section of space. Moments later, the creatures jumped out of warp and began to pursue the ship.

"Evasive maneuvers! Fire at will!" Stewart shouted.

In Sickbay, James felt the ship fall out of warp. There was a momentary pause, followed by the ship's sudden and irregular movements. Both the wounded and the medics in Sickbay were thrown around as the ship shifted violently. The patient with the broken rib fell off the bed and onto the exposed bone jutting out of his torso. He let out a blood-curdling cry.

The sounds of weapons being fired prompted James to sprint back to the bridge. He reached the bridge out of breath. "Report!" he gasped.

"Sir, a group of Cyclops jumped into warp with us and attacked us," Stewart stated. "*Kratos* was caught unaware and has been destroyed."

"Fire everything you've got at them!" James ordered, "Pallas, scan all nearby regions for geographical anomalies."

"There is a red giant star, a Class 4 nebula, and an asteroid belt within short range," the computer said immediately.

"Give me more details about the Class 4 nebula."

"Protosolar Class 4 Nebula has a strong positive electric charge and receives frequent bursts of lightning."

James gave a quick nod. "Set a course for that nebula, and get us there fast," he told Eli.

"Sir, the nebula will fry our circuitry," Stewart pointed out.

"That's what I'm counting on," James replied grimly.

Nike moved at maximum speed for the nebula. The Cyclops followed in close pursuit. The screen showed eight AI creatures, and each of them was almost twice the size of the first creature they had encountered.

"We're not going to make it—warp us within 1,000 kilometers of the nebula!" James shouted.

"Yes, sir!" Eli replied. *Nike* jumped into warp, on course to reach the nebula in a matter of minutes.

The Cyclops followed along the same warp stream, getting closer by the second. Just as one of them was about to reach *Nike*, the ship jumped out of warp. The Cyclops did so a second later.

The nebula was large and stretched farther than the eye could see, an enormous dusty purple cloud floating in space with tiny electric sparks twinkling in the debris.

"Full speed ahead," James ordered. "When we reach the perimeter, cut all electric power. Once we enter the nebula, thrusters only."

"Aye, sir," Eli said, executing his commands on the navigation panel.

The deck was silent as they entered the nebula—there was a sense that so much as a sneeze might set off an electrical reaction. The band of Cyclops followed until they reached the nebula's edge. One creature tested its perimeter, gingerly dipping a tentacle into the purple haze. At first, nothing happened, so it cautiously proceeded to venture into the nebula. Ten yards into the purple debris, little shocks began zapping the creature, reacting to its electrical circuitry. The creature retreated; all of the others backed away from the nebula, too. All, that is, but one, which seemed not to have any concern for its own safety. Consumed with a thirst for revenge, a lone Cyclops sped after James' ship.

"Sir, there's one in pursuit," Rumi said from the surveillance panel.

"That's suicide," James muttered in disbelief.

"Probably. But that might not stop it from destroying us first," Stewart said, looking apprehensively at the screen.

The Cyclops was moving swiftly through the nebula. Little shocks zapped against its metal exterior as it passed through the electrically charged dust. The electric shocks slowed it down, but it kept pressing forward relentlessly.

"That's one damn stubborn vacuum!" Drew commented.

"Evasive maneuvers!" James shouted as the Cyclops got within striking distance. *Nike* bobbed and weaved in response as the Cyclops lunged with its tentacles outstretched. Its mechanical mandibles opened wide to consume the ship.

The crew braced for impact. Ken crossed himself, muttering a prayer under his breath. Even James clenched his jaw, preparing for impact and expecting the worst. He had been close to death several times before, but never before had he had the feeling that it was "the end." In his mind, he began praying to God, to the spirits around him, to the universe, to anyone who might be listening to save him and let him live to make it home and see his family again.

Suddenly, a buildup of highly charged electrical particles formed a lightning bolt that struck the Cyclops. The creature went lifeless, floating like a dead metal jellyfish in murky waters. The crew could scarcely believe their luck.

"Continue on thrusters only," James said, unable the hide the relief in his voice. "Let's keep going to the other side of the nebula. Hopefully, the creatures will get tired of waiting and go home."

With a newfound energy, Eli said, "Yes, sir. Plotting a course through the nebula. Thrusters only."

James let out a sigh as he plopped down into his chair. In those final moments, he had fully expected to perish. All he could think about was his wife and son and how he'd never see them again. *I have to get home*, he thought resolutely.

All of the lights were still out on the ship except for the low-level lights illuminating the floors and consoles. James was still running on adrenaline. He sprang up to pace the floor, half-expecting to for another catastrophe to hit at any moment.

"Scan the nebula for any abnormalities," he ordered. "We've been taken by surprise twice now—I want to know if anything else is out there."

"Copy that," Stewart said. He quickly walked over to the surveillance console to consult with Rumi. They pulled up multiple feeds—audio, visual, radio wave, microwave, and ultraviolet data—then sorted through it. Rumi noticed something and pointed it out to Stewart.

Stewart appeared perplexed as he tried to understand what he was seeing. "Sir," Stewart said, "I think you need to see this."

James walked over to the panel showing the nebula. Rumi zoomed in over a small moving object. As the object grew in size, it became apparent that it was a junk spacecraft moving slowly through the debris.

"It appears they've turned off their power as well—they're barely moving," Rumi said.

"Sir," Francis interjected, "we're getting an incoming message."

"From whom?" James asked.

"It appears the junk ship, sir," Francis said as surprised as the rest of them.

"Put it up on the screen." James was more than a little curious.

CHAPTER 9:

ATARA

A video message appeared on the central screen. It showed a tall, svelte alien female with large feline eyes. Spots descended down either side of her cheeks, neck, and torso, and she was dressed in a dark, form-fitting uniform. A few disarmingly beautiful female aliens flanked her, dressed in similarly form-hugging uniforms.

"Greetings," she said. "My name is Captain Atara, and I am in command of this humble junk ship. My crew and I were commissioned to retrieve and recycle space junk in this quadrant when we were attacked by AI creatures. We barely escaped into this nebula with our lives. It appears you've encountered the same predators. We'd like to invite you onboard to regroup and discuss working together to escape."

The men on the deck stared at the screen as if they hadn't seen a female in years. Many of the young cadets had left for Hectar never having had a girlfriend back home. The Stellaes had made a collective decision to only bring male soldiers and scientists to battle. Not because women were less capable, but due to the long travel time— it took about a year to get to Hectar and another to get back—they didn't want any fraternization resulting in unwanted pregnancies in space.

"Prepare a message saying that we accept their invitation, then set a course to rendezvous with them on their current course," James said.

"Sir, I must strongly object," Stewart interjected.

"They're in the same predicament we are. We'll be stronger together than on our own," James countered.

Stewart shook his head. "They're an unknown. In the past 24 hours, we've been attacked twice and lost three ships, four if you count having to abandon *Athena*. With all due respect, sir, while these aliens appear to be friendly, we can't discount the very real possibility that they are hostile and this is a trap."

"Noted." James considered both possibilities. "Perhaps this is a risk," he conceded. "But then again, we might be taking a chance if we don't band together with them—after all, there is strength in numbers. And even if we decide not to work together, they might know something about the AI creatures that could be helpful. So far, we haven't done so well on our own."

He looked around the deck to gauge the attitude of his crew and saw that most seemed to agree. Although the ship was not run democratically, still, James liked to take the opinions of his crewmembers into account whenever he could. "Stewart, assemble a light crew. You'll lead the expedition yourself—your skepticism will be an asset."

Stewart nodded in reluctant agreement. He choose a few cadets to make up the team and walked off the bridge.

"Set a course to rendezvous with the junk ship," James said as he watched the men leave the deck.

Stewart, Drew, and ten cadets headed to the cargo bay and boarded a shuttle. The shuttle slipped quietly and slowly into the nebula using only its thrusters.

Onboard, the mood was quiet and ominous. One of the younger cadets, Panor, was nervously bouncing his knees. The anxious cadet couldn't get the image of the Cyclops destroying the ship out of his head. Still, he had a giddy feeling, a jittery electric excitement, as he thought about Atara and her appealing crew.

When they got within close range, two large doors leading to the junk ship's cargo bay opened. The shuttle swooped in. After the doors had closed and the room was pressurized, Stewart and his crew exited their shuttle into the junk's cargo bay. They were greeted by Atara and a few alien female crewmembers.

Atara stepped forward. "Welcome. I am Atara, the captain of this recycling vessel."

"Thank you for the invitation," Stewart responded. "I am first officer Stewart. We were on route to our home planet when we were attacked by a band of AI creatures, and we took harbor in this nebula."

"As did we," Atara said. She stepped in closer and lightly grasped Stewart's arm. "But all of that can wait. We've prepared some refreshments to welcome you, as is our custom. Let's share stories after we've had a drink. Then we can discuss next steps." She released him and started walking towards the corridor. The other crew hesitated momentarily, then followed Atara and Stewart.

As they walked down the corridor, the men looked around, taking in the strange surroundings, or at least what they could see of it—the only lighting was dim glow lights that accented the perimeters of walls and floors. The interior of the ship seemed to be primarily made of rough, recycled metals in dark shades of rusty reds and browns that seemed to absorb the surrounding light. Bits and pieces of space junk had been soldered together to form storage bins, doors, sitting areas, and consoles. They passed several open doors and tried to peer in. One revealed a storage area; another, a scrap room.

Farther down the corridor, they entered a large mess hall. Long tables had been set up buffet-style, offering an assortment of appetizing dishes: skewers with large chunks of fire-roasted meat, hot bread brushed with oil, a variety of sweet and savory dips, little pastries with crushed nuts on top, and roasted black beet-like vegetables.

The beet-like vegetables appeared to be bleeding—a thick red liquid pooled beneath them on the white serving platters.

Huge jugs of a sparkling red alcoholic beverage were being mixed in large bowls. The alien women ladled it from the bowls and into small cups and passed them around. Smaller tables, benches, and chairs with cushions had been placed around the room in a semi-circular configuration.

"Make yourselves comfortable," Atara said, addressing the group.

"Captain, Atara—" Stewart began.

"Please, just call me Atara," she interrupted him. She smiled, coyly taking Stewart's arm and leading him over to the buffet.

He stubbornly stuck to the topic at hand. "When you encountered the AI creatures, were you able to disarm them?"

She paused to reflect. "Unfortunately, no. We were attacked by one and we tried to fight back, but after throwing everything we had at it, the creature still seemed unharmed. We fled to this nebula and have been hiding here for the past week. We thought that eventually, it would give up waiting for us to emerge." She smiled at him. "But then you showed up. Maybe we can leave together—safety in numbers!" She ran her fingers along Stewart's arm.

Stewart felt a jolt of electricity as Atara toyed with him; he became acutely aware of the heat radiating from her skin against his own. Her enchanting jasmine-cinnamon perfume made his insides flutter and his head feel light. Her unusually large feline-like gray eyes made Atara look innocent, but still, Stewart thought there was something mischievous in her expression just below the surface.

"We certainly would like to explore that option," he said politely, removing his arm from her grasp to take a drink off a tray. "If we exit the nebula together and flying in formation, then even if the creatures detect us, we'll have a better chance of getting away."

"I like the way you think!" Atara said. She picked up a glass of her own and toasted him.

Stewart was about to take a sip of his drink when something curious caught his eye. A young cadet, Jin, was guzzling a pitcher of the sparkling drink. The bubbly liquid was seeping out of the sides of his mouth, soiling his clothes and pooling on the floor.

"Excuse me a moment," Stewart apologized to Atara. He put down his drink and walked over to Jin.

"What's going on, cadet?" Stewart said sternly. Without his noticing, a rhythmic song had started playing in the background.

"Nothing, sir," Jin said dismissively. He wiped his mouth on his sleeve, walked past Stewart, and started dancing.

Stewart turned, tracking him, and saw that several cadets were clapping along to the beat and watching an alien girl dance in the middle of the room. A handful of cadets got up to dance with her while others hedonistically devoured plates heaped with food and downed large cups of the sparkling beverage.

Stewart turned slowly in a circle, shocked but not entirely surprised. All around him, the men were starting to act rowdy. It appeared that Atara's crew was encouraging the cadets to eat and drink but were not eating or drinking themselves—although some held drinks or plates of food, none of the women had consumed so much as a morsel. After what had happened on Decta, Stewart was more than a little suspicious.

He walked over to Panor, who was standing on a table. "Get down at once! What's gotten into you?" Stewart shouted over the music.

Panor ignored him. An alien handed him a large pitcher of a bubbly brew, and the cadet started to chug it amid rowdy cheers coming around the room. Atara watched calmly from a distance.

Another cadet was eating a large plate of meat skewers with his hands. He had dipping sauce smeared across his cheeks, but he wasn't stopping to wipe his face—instead, he continued to ravage the skewers with an animalistic hunger. Two alien crewmembers sat on either side of him, stroking his shoulders and back like he was a pet.

Another cadet was dancing as a female alien tossed bite-sized pastries into his mouth. Stewart did a double-take when he noticed two cadets kissing and groping alien crewmembers.

Perhaps due to the intense stress of the situation—or maybe it was the strange aromas of the alien cuisine—Stewart began to feel that the room was swirling around him. He shouted to his men to return to his ship.

None of them paid any attention. Across the room, the intoxicated Panor fell off the table. It looked as though he had broken his neck, Stewart saw with horror. He rushed over to help, but was too late—the cadet was dead.

Stewart looked around and saw that one by one, his men were losing their self-control. The alien women were laughing and appeared to be enjoying watching the men give in to their basest desires. One alien girl slapped a cadet on the rear. He grunted, pulled off his uniform, and bent over for more. The girls all laughed hysterically.

Only Atara remained calm and dethatched, if not jaded. Stewart realized he was helpless to save his men. He didn't know what was wrong with the cadets, but he was sure he'd need help to deal with the insanity that was occurring. Amidst all the chaos, he quietly snuck out unnoticed and returned to the shuttle.

Stewart's shuttle sped back to *Nike*. He landed in the cargo bay, stumbled out of the shuttle, and sprinted all the way to the bridge. When he made it there, he was so distraught that he was barely able to get a word out. He scarcely managed to hand a napkin containing a food sample to the science officer, Rajeev, before he collapsed into the first officer's chair.

"Analyze that food sample!" he managed to gasp. "I'm not sure how, but I think the food is altering the cadets' impulse control."

James came over and knelt down next to Stewart. "What the hell happened down there? Where's the rest of the crew?"

As Stewart recounted all that had transpired onboard Atara's ship, Rajeev wasted no time in analyzing the food sample. "Interesting," he said, looking up from his console. "The sample contains a compound that can potentially transform humanoid DNA. It will require further analysis, but it would appear that the first officer's hypothesis could be correct."

"Can you synthesize an antidote?" James asked.

Rajeev paused, his eyebrows pulling together in concentration. "I don't know," he finally said. "That could take quite some time to design." His tone shifted from hesitant to determined. "But I'll get started, sir, and let you know what I come up with." He stood, placing the sample in a clear container, and headed for the research lab located on a lower deck.

Stewart sank into his chair, burying his head in his hands. James tried to put a hand on his shoulder, but Stewart brushed it away. James had never seen Stewart so distraught. His first officer was normally so highly logical and pragmatic that James had wondered for years if Stewart had normal emotional responses at all.

Regardless of Stewart's state of mind, though, James knew he couldn't leave the cadets on Atara's ship. He remained silent for several minutes, deliberating as to how to proceed. "I'm going to that ship, and I'm going to get our men back," he finally said. Resolve had hardened his voice.

Stewart looked up. "No, you can't go back there! Not alone, anyway—we need to get our men back by force."

"No," James disagreed, shaking his head. "I can't put the entire ship at risk. Especially in this nebula—trying to mount any confrontation with *Nike's* weapons could be deadly. It's best if I go by myself and try diplomacy."

Stewart kept objecting, but despite his pleading, James remained adamant. "As captain, it's my duty and obligation. Stewart, you have the bridge." James turned and headed for the cargo bay.

Given no other option, Stewart pulled himself together. "Francis, scan Atara's ship for any type of communications. Let's see if we can find any clues."

"Aye, sir," Francis said.

"Thomas, analyze Atara's ship for any mechanical weaknesses or flaws in her design. We may need to stage a rescue mission, and I'll need a point of entry."

"Yes, sir," Thomas replied.

"Ken, pull up anything we know about Atara's people: religious practices, history, customs. Anything and everything. If there's something that might be helpful for the captain, we need it ASAP."

"On it, sir!" Ken said.

James was halfway to the cargo bay when Rajeev came running after him. "Stop, captain! Wait!" Rajeev shouted.

James stopped in his tracks; Rajeev was soon standing in front of him.

"I have a vaccine of sorts," Rajeev said haltingly, out of breath. "I ran the sample through the lab's DNA sequencing program. It turns out that the active compound—a complex protein in the food—targets the mitochondrial DNA and uses that as an entryway to alter DNA sequencing. The compound damages the gene responsible for impulse control, rendering a person unable to control themselves."

He took another big lungful of air, then continued. "Stewart was right, sir—the men will do the first thing that comes to mind. And it gets worse. If any suggestion enters their subconscious, they'll have no way to logically process it. You say 'Bark!' and they'll act like a hound."

He held up a vial with a small black pill in it. "I used the sequencing program to synthesize a mitochondrial DNA blocker. Take this, and it will render the substance ineffective." He handed the container to James.

"So you're saying that I can eat and drink the food and it will have no effect on me?" James asked, his eyebrows raised.

"I'm not 100% sure this will work, sir," Rajeev said apologetically. "I haven't had time to run enough tests, and there could be other attributes I haven't accounted for. But to the best of my knowledge, after taking this, the food and drink will not affect you—you'll still have your normal level of self-control."

"Thank you, Rajeev," James said gratefully, slapping Rajeev on the back and squeezing his arm firmly. He knew Rajeev and Jin had been in a not-so-secret relationship for several years, so getting the cadets back safe and sound was especially meaningful for Rajeev.

James opened the vial, popped the pill into his mouth, tilted his head back, and swallowed it. "It will be effective in 30 minutes and should last up to four hours, so don't consume any food before or after that time," Rajeev instructed.

James patted him again on the shoulder and then resumed his trek to the cargo bay. "I'll get them home!" he shouted without looking back.

As he prepared to take off, James heard from the bridge. "We did some research on Atara's cultural and religious practices, captain," Stewart said. "The females on her planet enslaved the men centuries ago. They felt the men were reprehensibly self-centered and were pushing their planet past a sustainable carbon footprint towards the point of no return. After turning the male population into slaves with the same chemical that made our men susceptible to any suggestion, they restored environmental balance. For all intensive purposes, the male population is kept essentially as pets and slaves to do the female's bidding. However, it turns out that Atara's people, the Catarans, are very religious—they place a lot of cultural significance on keeping oaths. If you can force her to promise something on her gods, most likely she'll keep her word."

James smiled tightly. "It's better than nothing. Let's pray that works!"

He sped off in the shuttle and docked in Atara's ship. Atara and several of her crewmembers greeted him in the cargo bay. "Welcome to our humble recycling ship," she said with a friendly smile. "I'm Captain Atara."

James stepped forward. "I'm Captain James Odysseus, and I've come to retrieve my men," he said firmly.

"Yes, of course," Atara said in a disingenuous tone. "Your men are fine—they are resting now. First, let's share some refreshments. It is our custom."

"Very well," James said stiffly. "After you."

Atara led James to the mess hall. As he followed her through the dark corridors, he wondered if he was making a mistake. What if the pill didn't work? What if this was a pointless exercise and he'd end up just like the cadets? Still, he felt like he had to give it a try—he knew they'd do the same for him.

As they passed the mess hall, in place of the lavish arrangement Stewart had told him about, James saw only a dark metal table and a single cushioned couch. The celebratory mess hall must have been set up just for his crew, he realized. Nonetheless, Atara led him into the hall and gestured for him to sit.

A crewmember promptly brought over a plate heaped high with skewered meats, sweet pastries, and dips while another girl served the bubbly drink, pouring it from pitchers into tall glasses. James hesitated momentarily before taking a bite of the food and a sip of the drink. *There's no turning back now,* he thought grimly.

Atara appeared pleased. James felt rather apprehensive and carefully monitored himself for any changes. After a few minutes, Atara moved in closer to examine him.

She swept his hair away from his ears. "Take off your clothes," she said playfully.

"No," James replied, relieved that her suggestion had no impact on him.

She looked mildly alarmed. "You need some more to drink," Atara said. She stood and raised a hand to signal for another glass.

James shot upright and caught her by the wrist. "I've had enough."

"What are you?" Atara blurted out, clearly surprised. "No man has ever refused me!"

In response, James tightened his grip on her wrist and twisted it behind her back. He grabbed the knife off the table and held it to her throat. "Like I said, I am Captain James Odysseus. You will reverse what you did to my men and you will return them to me. If you do that, I'll let you live."

Fear and confusion flashed across Atara's face. Her crewmembers rushed in to help, but James pressed the knife in deeper, slicing through the first layer of her spotted neck. Black blood trickled down over her collarbone.

The others stopped in their tracks, afraid to cause the death of their beloved leader. "Alright, alright, I will return your men to you!" Atara gasped.

James continued. "And you must swear an oath on your gods that you will not harm us in any way."

Without hesitating, Atara said, "Yes, this I promise as well."

He removed the blade from her throat. As soon as he did, Atara leaned in and kissed him passionately. James felt the urge to kiss her back—there was something intoxicating about her spotted skin, big eyes, and alien perfume—but he was also afraid of Atara. She reminded him of a deadly insect that would lure in a male and mate with him, only to reward him by biting off his head. Also, he knew Ella was waiting for him.

James pulled away from her. "Just return my men, and we'll be on our way," he said firmly.

"As you wish," Atara replied. She looked at her crewmembers. "Bring the holy root, boil it into juice, and offer it to the men."

The girls left and returned in short order with a large plant that had a black root and a milk-white flower. They placed it in a large pot of boiling water. After boiling it, they poured the purple fluid into pitchers and nodded at Atara.

James followed Atara and her crewmembers to the quarters where the men were being held. He couldn't believe his eyes: his men were sleeping soundly on the filthy floor, lying next to garbage and animal droppings. He had to cover his nose with his sleeve to avoid the rank smell.

Two girls walked around with the pitcher. "Wake up," one said as she squatted next to one of the cadets. He opened his eyes and sat up immediately. "Drink this," she said, handing him a glass of the purple drink.

The cadet obediently downed the drink. The girls repeated this with the others until all of the men were feeling more like themselves. James was relieved to see the crew up and about again. He wasn't sure if they were back to their normal selves or not, but he wasn't going to stick around to find out. "Let's go!" he barked at them, and they sprang up to follow him out of the disgusting room.

They hurried back to the shuttle and then flew to the ship with as much decorum as was possible after such an ordeal. They were met on *Nike* with cheers, hugs, and applause. Stewart felt ashamed that he had run, but the men hailed him as a hero—had he not had the wherewithal to bring back a sample of the food, the cadets might all still be slaves to Atara and her crewmembers. The cadets raised James and Stewart up on their shoulders, cheering and parading them around the corridors.

In the midst of the celebrations, Jin snuck away to find Rajeev in the laboratory, where he was still examining the food specimen. Jin walked in quietly and put his hands over Rajeev's eyes as he was looking through a microscope.

Rajeev turned around, knowing Jin's hands immediately. He could scarcely contain his joy. The lovers embraced one another, kissing passionately.

Jin wiped Rajeev's tears away as they trickled down his cheeks. "I thought I'd lost you," Rajeev whispered, barely able to get the words out.

"I'd never leave you," Jin reassured him.

On the bridge, James turned to Eli. "Get us the hell out of here! Thrusters only until we exit the nebula, then maximum warp."

"With pleasure, sir," Eli said, tapping away at the navigation console.

CHAPTER 10

THE OWELLIS

The crew felt nervous as they exited the nebula, half-expecting a Cyclops to appear at any moment. "Resuming course for Earth at maximum warp," Eli said.

The computer's voice rang out: "Initiating warp protocol in 10, 9, 8, 7, 6, 5, 4, 3, 2, 1..." James and the rest of the crew braced themselves as the ship jumped into warp in a swirl of light. Everyone settled in and began monitoring their progress.

Given what they had been through and what they were still up against on their voyage home, James was worried they wouldn't make it. He stood and addressed everyone on deck. "We have only one ship left, and many unknowns lie between us and our objective," he said without preamble. "We'll be greatly outnumbered and outgunned should we encounter a hostile species. What are our options for getting back home more quickly?"

The deck was quiet as the crew pondered alternatives. Finally, Eli cleared his throat and spoke up. "Sir, there is a wormhole not far from here. It could potentially take us 80% of the journey in a matter of minutes."

"It's also very risky," Stewart interjected. "Wormholes are notoriously unpredictable. One time you exit in one quadrant; the next time you go through, you might be on the other side of the galaxy."

Eli spoke up again, undeterred. "This happens to be one of the more predictable wormholes," he pointed out. "It has a 60% consistency rate."

Stewart gave him a hard look. "That's a 40% chance we might end up God knows where or when." One of the blood vessels on the first officer's forehead looked as though it might burst.

"Considering what we're up against, I think we had better take those odds," James broke in. "A 60% chance of us shaving off a huge chunk of our voyage home and getting out of range of those damn AIs sounds pretty good to me."

Stewart shook his head. "Again, sir, I must strongly object. There's no way of knowing how this will turn out."

James paused. He knew Stewart might be right, but he also wanted to get home as soon as possible. He felt there was an element of unknown risk either way, and at least the wormhole had a good chance of reducing their travel time. "Noted," he said decisively. "I believe this is our best course of action. Cadet, set a course for the wormhole."

"Aye, sir. Setting a route now," Eli replied.

The ship shifted slightly underneath them. "Estimated travel time is 4 hours and 23 minutes," the computer said.

Rajeev, who had resumed his post on the bridge a few minutes earlier, began researching the wormhole. He looked up from his console and said, "Sir, reports of this wormhole indicate it is a home to four-dimensional creatures that supposedly 'sing.' They are called the Owellis."

James and the rest of the crew looked puzzled. "And why is the singing important?" James asked.

Rajeev also looked confused by what he was seeing. "Apparently, sir, these beings are able to induce a trance-like state through their soundwaves. Those who listen to their 'song' experience the past, present, and future simultaneously, and they try to remain in the wormhole, where they eventually die of madness, exposure, or starvation."

Rajeev's expression was getting more and more apprehensive as he went on. "Entire ships have been lost. Those who listen to the song forget their purpose and do not wish to return home." He looked up at James. "All crewmembers must wear noise-canceling earbuds for protection."

"See to it," James replied. The crew had to take all possible precautions, of course, but something about the four-dimensional creatures spoke to him. He could feel a giddy curiosity welling up in his chest. *What would it feel like to listen to their singing?* he couldn't help but wonder.

While Rajeev and his science team hurried to pass out earbuds to all onboard the ship, James came up with a plan to hear the song and live to tell about it. First, he commanded his crew to restrain him in his captain's chair by tying him to his seat and erecting a force field around him. Stewart would command the ship until they were safely through the wormhole.

"I'd tell you that I don't think this is a good idea, but I can see your mind is already made up," Stewart said.

James gave him a slight smile. "You know me so well! You'd think we'd been to the other side of the galaxy and back together."

"We're not back, yet, sir," Stewart retorted dryly before he turned to address the bridge.

"Regardless of what the captain might say as we pass through the wormhole, you are under orders to ignore him—you are to go about your duties until we have made it through to the other side," he reminded them all.

Some of the cadets anxiously looked to James for reassurance. James nodded. "You heard the man! Listen to your commanding officer."

The ship jumped out of warp and approached a seemingly empty quadrant of space. *Nike* slowed to a stop.

"Sir, we have arrived at the wormhole coordinates," Eli said.

The first officer gave him a nod of acknowledgment, then tapped his earbuds. "To all crew," he said, addressing everyone through their earbuds, "we are about to enter the wormhole. Keep your earbuds in until we have safely passed through. You will be able to hear one another and communicate through the earbuds, but you will not hear any outside noise."

He looked at Rajeev, eyebrows raised. "All scans indicate the wormhole is functioning normally, sir," Rajeev reported.

"Proceed," Stewart said.

The ship moved forward slowly. With a flash of light, the wormhole opened, revealing an illuminated swirling tunnel cutting through space-time. *Nike* entered and the wormhole closed.

Inside the wormhole, it was both bright and dark at the same time. The wormhole appeared to spin around the ship as it passed through; light and dark spots streamed through viewports and bounced off the walls of corridors and rooms. With its wide viewscreens, the bridge was particularly affected.

James sat alert in his chair, listening for the sounds of the Owellis. An insatiable curiosity was eating away at his insides.

"Monitor all frequencies. Keep moving ahead at a steady pace," Stewart said.

A high-pitched, piercing noise rang out in the background, but only James noticed. It faded into lulling tones. "It's so beautiful!" he gasped. Voices echoed in his ears. "Did you hear that?" he asked the bridge at large.

No one paid any attention to him. "Come with us!" the voices whispered.

"The voices! Can you hear them?" James shouted, looking around.

Rajeev glanced at James and shook his head, pointing to his earbuds to indicate that he couldn't hear a thing.

"Need I remind you of your orders?" Stewart's stern voice came through the earbuds and cut into the beguiling voices in James' head. "Pay no attention to the captain under any circumstances! Man your station until we are through this wormhole."

Everyone hunched over their consoles and studiously ignored James.

James leaned back in his chair as the whispering got louder. "So much beauty…" he muttered, closing his eyes. Suddenly, he was transported to a memory in the past, a moment in time very dear to him.

He was standing in a sun-filled room. He saw Ella sitting up in a hospital bed, holding newborn baby Max in her arms and beaming with joy. James ran his fingers through her hair and kissed her affectionately, wondering how she could look so radiant only hours after having given birth.

He bent over and kissed little baby Max on the forehead, inhaling a deep breath of intoxicating new-baby smell. Then he scooped Max up in his arms, cradling the swaddled infant, feeling the warmth of his delicate little body against his chest. *How is this possible?* he wondered in a corner of his mind. *How am I again at the birth of my son?*

Although it didn't seem possible, it felt amazingly real; he was so overwhelmingly happy that he hardly had space to pause and think. The exuberant experience of being with his wife and son flooded him with joy.

All of a sudden, James was jarringly transported to a memory of Hectar. "And then there's pain… So much suffering," he heard the voices say.

He found himself onboard the Hectaran home-ship. Explosions were going off everywhere. A man on fire ran screaming down the corridor; the scent of burning flesh lingered in the air. James felt sick to his stomach amidst all the death and destruction.

"What am I doing here?" James asked the voices.

There was no answer. James felt his entire body go weak as he was forced to watch more of the horrific scene.

Then, suddenly, he was transported to another place, one he did not recognize. An escape pod crash-landed in a grassy meadow.

"Why? Why do you go here?" the voices whispered.

From a distance, James saw himself stumble out of the pod, barely making it out in time before the pod exploded. James was very confused. *When did this happen?* He had no recollection of the crash, but somehow it felt familiar, like it was something yet to come. His head felt light, and his body felt like it was floating.

James had barely had a moment to make sense of what he had seen before he was transported to another place. He found himself on a familiar cliff on Ithaca, engulfed in a pervasive gray fog. An old man stood at the edge of the abyss. The old man turned around slowly, and James realized he was looking at a much older version of himself. *I must be in the future, visiting memories yet to be made,* he realized. *In the wormhole, the Orwellis experience past, present, and future simultaneously...*

His future self had entirely white hair and a shaggy, long beard. "Why would you go here when you could stay with us?" the voices taunted him. "Stay with us where it's so beautiful..." The voices ran over one another in a hypnotic harmony.

James was back at the wedding of Xing-Xing and Dave, once again dancing with Ella. He pulled her in close, his hand around her waist. He breathed in her delicate scent as he felt her soft skin against his stubbly cheek.

He realized that his head was starting to pound; dark red blood began trickling out of his nose. He wiped it away with his wrist, not wanting to be distracted even for a moment from being in this bliss-ful moment with Ella.

On the bridge, although the crew was under strict orders to ignore the restrained captain, several glanced over at him nervously. James' eyes were closed, but a little blood seeped out of his left nostril. It appeared that he was dreaming or in a trance. He was also mumbling something undecipherable.

He tossed and turned, pushing against his restraints. Suddenly, he screamed out, "Let me stay here! Leave me here! It's so beautiful… Please leave me here!"

Stewart pursed his lips and gave each of the crew a stern look. "You have your orders, cadets! Ignore the captain and focus on getting us the hell out of here."

James opened his eyes, still thrashing violently in his chair. He wanted desperately to stay in the wormhole. Where they were bound to his chair, his arms were beginning to bleed as he fought his restraints. Then his eyes closed again.

Within his mind, James stood alone in a glowing white incandescent hall. "Where am I?" he asked.

"Why do you keep coming here?" the voices sang to him in a hoarse whisper.

Suddenly James was back on Atara's ship, seeing the cadets huddled in the filthy room. James rushed over to help, but the image suddenly dissipated, and he was back on the Hectaran home-ship. The interior walls of the great sphere were burning, and terrifying screams of women and children could be heard over the crackling flames. His head and stomach hurt terribly, making him double over in pain.

"It's in the past!" James shouted. "I had no choice in this! Take me back to her!"

In a flash, he was in the bedroom he had shared with Ella, and the two of them were cuddling in bed. He pulled the sheets over their heads as the early morning sun seeped into the room. James reveled in the sweetness of her smile and the way her eyes twinkled with a playful mischievousness. Her wavy auburn hair glowed red in the sunlight.

She giggled and tried to wiggle away as he tickled her. He stopped and kissed her shoulder, running his hand down her back. "Stay here with us," the voices whispered.

"Stay with me, James," Ella said to him. "Never leave!"

"Yes," James answered. "Yes, I'll stay here with you." He felt like he would never tire of looking deep into Ella's green eyes.

On the bridge, turbulence started to jostle the ship. "Exiting the wormhole in 1,000 meters!" Eli shouted over the sounds of the ship.

"What's causing the turbulence?" Stewart asked.

"Unclear, sir," Eli said, shaking his head as his fingers skittered over his console.

"It could be interference from the four-dimensional creatures, or it could be that the wormhole exits at a location next to a strong gravitational force," Rajeev offered.

"All crew on high alert!" Stewart shouted.

James' eyes opened again, and he screamed, "Noooooo!! Don't leave the wormhole. Leave me here! I want to stay. I want to stay with her!!" He managed to rip off his restraints, and then he stood and started throwing himself into the force field. It held, but he threw himself against it again and again, like a crazed animal trying to escape.

"Exiting the wormhole in 10, 9, 8, 7, 6, 5, 4, 3, 2, 1..." the computer blandly stated.

A flash of light surrounded the ship, and they were back in normal space.

CHAPTER II

SYCOON AND CHOOMTRA

Hardly had their eyes adjusted to leaving the incredibly bright and then painfully dark wormhole when they realized there was a new blinding brightness. The ship had exited the wormhole in close proximity to two massive stars spinning around one another.

Stewart lowered the force field surrounding James. The captain was groggy, but it was clear he was returning to his normal self once again. He rubbed his head, realizing he had a terrible headache.

"Report," the first officer said.

"The wormhole opened up in an unexpected location," Eli responded. "We're next to two supermassive stars, Sycoon and Choomtra, and we're being pulled into their gravitational orbits."

"Full reverse! Get us out of here!" James barked.

"I'm trying, sir," Eli said. He was already maxing out the ship's thrusters, but *Nike* continued to be pulled in. "Sir, I'm giving it all we've got, but it's not enough—we're being sucked in!"

"Warp us out of here!" James shouted.

"Sir, we can't," Thomas cut in. "The radiation from the two stars is interfering with our warp core, making it go temporarily offline."

"Well, get it back! We didn't make it all this way to burn up in binary stars!" James commanded.

Rajeev threw in a suggestion. "Sir, although we might not be able to escape their mass, we might be able to go right between them and escape on the other side." He put up a holographic chart of the massive binary stars, using it to point out the suggested route.

"We are here," Rajeev said as he pointed to a coordinate. "Given our proximity to Sycoon, we can't escape her gravitational force, no. But if we lean into her gravitational pull, we can start an orbital trajectory that would put us on a path here—" he pointed again— "that we could follow to cut between the stars. If we stay on that course, according to my calculations, we have a 50% probability of making it through." Although his voice was calm, his hands were shaking, James noticed.

"And if we don't make it through?" Stewart asked.

Rajeev looked grim. "The binary stars will either pull us apart at the seams or one of them will suck us in and we'll burn up," he answered bluntly.

The bridge crew was silent as mental images of the disastrous outcomes churned through their minds. "That's the craziest idea I've ever heard, but we don't have any other options," James finally said. "Make it happen."

In response, Eli bent over his console and plotted a course that would take them between the massive binary stars.

"Maximum shields," James said, nodding at Eli.

Nike edged closer to the stars. Everyone was tense; one cadet puked on himself.

Nike continued to press on. The blinding light coming from the two stars forced the crew to avert their eyes from the screen. "Dim the screen," James ordered.

The intense heat of the stars started to break through the shields, damaging the exterior of the ship. *Nike* began to shake and rattle. Pieces of the exterior plating started flying off in multiple directions.

"Sir, the gravitational forces of the stars are pulling our ship in two directions," Rajeev said. "If we don't get through faster, we're going to be ripped in two." Beads of sweat collected on his brow, and he wiped them away with his sleeve.

Eli shouted, "I'm giving it all we've got, but it's not enough, sir!"

"We need the warp back online, NOW!" James shouted.

Thomas looked at him with panic in his eyes. "I'm sorry, captain, but there is nothing we can do—radiation has flooded the warp core, and it's even worse now than before. It will take days to restore it."

The ship shook harder as a deep rumble and a loud ripping sound permeated the hull.

An idea flashed through Stewart's mind. "If we abandon ship and detonate the core, the escape pods can bounce off the force of the ship exploding," he said excitedly. "It might be just enough to escape the gravitational forces and get us through and out the other side!"

On the face of it, Stewart's idea sounded absurd, but when James considered it, he realized this was the only possible way to save his crew. "Abandon ship!" James ordered.

There was a massive flurry of activity as the bridge crew rushed to obey his orders. The chief engineer prepped the core to detonate himself, then set the timer and headed for the escape pods. Cadets and bridge crew alike rushed through the corridors to close themselves off in pods, some doubling or tripling up as the ship was past capacity.

James couldn't believe what was happening. His head still hurt from his experience of passing through the wormhole, he hadn't had time to process what he'd seen, and now he was losing the last of his ships. He did his best to hold himself together.

"To all crew," he said on all-ship comms. "We are passing between two massive binary stars, and their gravitational forces are pulling our ship apart at the seams. We have one last shot at survival, but the timing must be precise in order for this plan to work. We will detonate the ship's core to provide a burst of energy that can push our escape pods past the gravitational pull of the stars. Again, I repeat, this has to be timed perfectly. The computer is calculating a count-down. Prepare to board the escape pods and follow the assigned trajectory for your pod. It has been an honor serving with you."

Only James and Stewart now remained on the bridge. "Time to disembark is two minutes. Counting down now..." the computer stated in its flat tone.

James and Stewart exchanged a look and a nod and then quickly exited the bridge and got into their pods as well. They made it just as they heard the final "4, 3, 2, 1..."

All of the pods disembarked in perfect unison at the same moment. A few seconds after the pods burst out, the ship's core exploded in a giant burst of energy. Parts of the ship ripped apart unexpectedly, hitting and destroying many of the pods. Others got pulled into the stars and burned up in a fiery trajectory.

James' pod was the only one to escape from the force of the explosion and shoot away from the stars, but just as he was almost clear, a small piece of shrapnel from the exploding ship hit his pod, damaging it.

James watched in disbelief as he saw *Nike* explode and his crew perish. Frantically, he pressed the communication controls. "James to crew! James to anyone! Anyone, come in!"

Radio silence. A secondary burst violently jolted the pod and threw James across the small space. He hit his head on the wall and was knocked unconscious. As he laid motionless on the floor, the computer initiated life-saving protocols and charted a course for the nearest Goldilocks land mass.

CHAPTER 12:

LENARA

The damaged pod progressed slowly through space, sparks trailing behind it as it sputtered on. It tried to send an SOS message, but its exterior hardware had melted and become inoperable. The pod neared the Lenara star and then approached a red-brown gas giant planet circled by several delicate rings and moons. It landed on one of the smaller moons that had an atmosphere humanoid life could inhabit.

James still lay unconscious on the floor. Through the ventilation system, the pod released a blast of adrenaline. James' eyes fluttered open.

He looked around at his damaged pod and slowly pushed himself into a sitting position. "Pallas, report," he croaked.

"Life-saving protocols were initiated when you were unconscious," the mechanical voice responded. "The pod has landed on a moon of a planet that is orbiting Lenara. The atmosphere of this moon is habitable."

James rubbed his head and felt dried blood caked into his hair. "Run a pod diagnostic," he grumbled.

It took a bit longer than usual for the computer to respond. "Power is at 10%; solar power is at 15%. Thrusters are damaged. Warp is intact. There is a minor hull breech."

James groaned as he staggered to his feet. "Show me a map! Where the hell are we?"

A holographic map appeared, and James examined it closely. "We're still 15 thousand light years from Earth," he muttered. Louder, he said, "Identify planets in close proximity that have humanoid life and whose inhabitants have developed warp capabilities."

Several points lit up on the hologram. "Pull up everything we know about these planets," he told the computer.

Information started feeding into a panel, and James sat down to start reading through it. He zoomed in on a picture of a mostly blue planet with a small green land mass: Scherie, home of the Ectarans. The Ectarans were an advanced peaceful humanoid civilization whose monarchs still presided over governmental, religious, and ceremonial duties. A millennia ago, the Ectarans had converted their energy sources into sustainable crystal-growing technologies, and they had been living in harmony with their environment ever since, at the same time growing rich on trade. They were renowned throughout the galaxy for their expertise in biochemistry, technology, and the arts.

His instincts told James that this was a planet whose inhabitants could assist him in returning to Earth. "Set a course for Scherie," he said to the computer.

"Unable to comply," the computer informed him. "Power levels are insufficient for takeoff."

"What power level is required for takeoff?" James asked.

"Power must be at a minimum of 30% or solar must be at 50%."

Anger welled up in him, and James kicked the wall so hard that he hurt his foot. He collapsed back into the chair, cradling his foot in his hands. "My kingdom for a solar battery!" he shouted.

"Unable to locate additional solar batteries," the computer replied.

James took a deep breath and forced himself into calmness. "Walk me through how to recharge them," he hissed through gritted teeth.

"First, remove the panel under the center console; next, remove the mobile solar charging panels. Then place the panels in direct sunlight," the computer explained.

James got down on his knees and removed the panel as instructed, fumbling with wires as he removed the solar batteries. All of his studies at the university, his training as a biological architect, his experience crossing the galaxy and fighting a war, and now his fate was dependent on his elementary mechanical skills… There was no one to whom he could vent his frustrations, so he bottled them up. His insides felt more and more like they were boiling over.

Finally, he had detached the solar panels. He got up and carried them to the door. When it opened, he saw a gray moon and gray desolate terrain stretching out endlessly. His heart felt heavy as he surveyed the bleak surroundings. The ground was sandy and dry, and faraway gray-brown hills lined the horizon. A dark, cloudy mist hovered in the sky, completely blocking the sun.

The solar batteries were designed to pick up light even in overcast climates, the computer had told him, but when he tested the air, he discovered that the clouds had a unique composition—they were heavy in iron and were blocking too much of the light for the battery to get a charge.

Perhaps it was foolish of him, but James still had hope. Maybe it was just a spell of bad weather and it would pass? He stepped out of the pod and removed a drone from his sack. He set it on the ground. "Survey the terrain," he said aloud. "Cover a fifty-kilometer radius surrounding the pod and report back."

The drone lifted off vertically and flew away to record the landscape.

James returned to his pod to observe the audio and visual drone feed on his computer screen. From the footage, he learned that the moon was covered in a thick atmosphere. Sunlight barely penetrated its surface, and when a few rays of sunlight did make it through the cloud layer, it didn't last long. Depressed and spent, James laid down and tried to sleep.

Days turned into weeks. James continued chasing after patches of sunlight to recharge the solar batteries whenever the drone found a location where the sun was breaking through the clouds. Usually, though, by the time he reached the indicated location, it was either gone or it dissipated soon after he arrived. The sunlight never lasted long enough to sufficiently charge the solar batteries to enable the pod to lift off the moon. However, here and there he'd catch enough light to keep his small devices running.

Weeks turned into months. James kept spending his days chasing sunlight and grieving for the loss of his crew. He felt like the universe was punishing him for his selfish desires. "Why??" he screamed at the sky. "Why take all of them and leave me?? My men had nothing to do with this. Punish *me*! Hurt *me*! Take *my* life!"

He took some comfort in suffering on a bleak and desolate hunk of dirt. *At least I'm paying penance for my sins*, he thought grimly. He collected water from moss on rocks in the hills and learned to farm, cook, and eat pond plankton. Many times, though, he longed for death to take him—he considered starvation, throwing himself off a cliff, or shooting himself with his own laser gun.

"There are worse ways to go," he'd tell himself late at night, when the winds howled like ravenous wolves around his pod and he couldn't sleep. Still, his intuition told him that the Universe, God, or some greater force had a purpose for him—his work in this life was not done yet. And the memories of his family and the hope of seeing Ella and Max again one day kept him going.

Months turned into years. By the sixth year, James was almost unrecognizable: he was dirty and disheveled, his uniform was stained and soiled, and his beard had grown long and wild. From time to time, he'd catch a few minutes of sunlight when Lenara's beautiful rays seeped through an opening in the clouds and warmed his heart, skin, and solar panels briefly before slipping away. "Lenara, you tease!" James would shout into the sky. "Is that all you've got? Come back here and show me what you're made of!" He started to worry that he was losing his mind.

One day, when he was taking apart a console in his pod and trying to reconfigure the wiring to make the pod more efficient, James came across an old-fashioned paper manual. He had forgotten that Ella had ordered one for each pod in case the computer system glitched and the passengers needed to figure out how to fix the pod. "Backups after backups!" she used to say. He had thought it was an unnecessary expense, but given that he was traveling halfway across the galaxy, he figured he would heed her little request if it in some way put her mind to rest.

Now James turned the manual into a journal, writing in the empty spaces, along the borders, and in between diagrams. It became his only companion besides the computer. Not only that, it reminded him of Ella—it gave him comfort to think that even if he died, one day she might find his journal and know his last thoughts.

One day on a whim, James decided to examine the planetary records of Lenara's solar system. He discovered that the magnetic field of the large gas giant planet was generated by the electrical currents in the planet's outer core. The moon that had become James' trap orbited the planet once every three Earth years.

An epiphany hit James. He calculated that there would be a magnetic anomaly when the moon spun around the planet's northernmost point. At a particular set of coordinates in 72 Earth hours, the cloud cover would be pulled back for a 24-hour window due to the heavy metal composition of the atmosphere.

He prayed his math was correct as he checked and rechecked his work, always arriving at the same conclusion. Finally, he collected the necessary supplies and made his way to the coordinates he had determined were correct.

The journey was long and hard, and James had to keep a steady pace to make it to his destination on time. On the first day, he hiked through the hills he had often stared at from the doorway of his pod. They were surprisingly steep and mostly barren and dry. Gray, dusty rock and dirt seemed to go on as far as the eye could see. Only moss and algae grew in the desolate climate, clinging to rocks in the shadowy crevices of the hills.

Halfway through the day, he started to get sharp pains in his side, but he stubbornly maintained his steady pace. He kept walking through sunset, when the sky turned black. The winds picked up. Grimly determined, he pressed on through the night, walking until his limbs were numb with exhaustion. Late into the night, James finally laid down next to a large stone to take refuge from the wind.

When his alarm woke him three hours later, he longed to rest a little longer. He knew, however, that if he fell asleep again, he might not make it to the coordinates in time, so he forced himself to his feet and continued onward.

The second day, when James realized the foothills were turning into mountains, his determination almost gave out. Looking up at the steep incline, he felt his knees wobble and his heart sink in his chest. As the altitude increased, the oxygen thinned out, making him short of breath. Still, he kept going, forcing himself to keep pace, fearing this was his last chance to return home. He doubted he could wait another three years for the moon to pass over the northern pole of the planet.

"I'd rather die trying to get there than go mad waiting another three years," James said to himself as bitter cold winds whipped around his face. His nose and cheeks turned red in the cold. He had wrapped scraps of cloth around his hands to protect his fingers from frostbite, but they felt almost as numb as his feet did. That night, he did not sleep at all—instead, he kept moving through the cold and dark for fear he might freeze to death if he tried to sleep.

On the third day, James reached the coordinates, a plateau at the edge of the mountains. He was a few hours ahead of schedule since he had pressed on through the darkness of the second night instead of resting. Seeing the plateau gave him a burst of fresh energy, and he set straight to work setting up his equipment and preparing the solar panels.

Then all there was to do was wait. He was half-excited and half-nervous. *What if my calculations are wrong? What if I'm in the wrong location? What if I calculated the time incorrectly?* James thought worriedly. He glanced at his tablet and the countdown ticking away. Every minute seemed to be an eternity. The countdown neared the end, and still there was no sign of sunlight. Finally, the timer ran out.

James stared at the sky, but it remained unchanged: a thick, gray, stubborn cloud formation still covered the entire atmosphere. Feeling defeated, he laid down on the hard surface of the plateau and closed his eyes. Tears started to run down his cheeks.

In the depth of his despair, James almost did not notice a subtle feeling of warmth on his neck, but then the warm feeling seemed to grow and move up to his jawline. He opened his eyes.

The clouds were parting; light was streaming through. A ray of sun was piercing through the cloud layer and falling directly on his face. James jumped to his feet and checked the equipment.

"Yes! Thank you, God! Thank you, Universe! Thank you, everyone and anyone out there!" James shouted at the top of his lungs. Gradually but steadily, the batteries absorbed the charge of the warm light of Lenara.

He reached his arms out wide to soak up the sun, feeling his skin tingle with its warmth. For the first time since he had landed on the moon, James felt happy. He looked over at his charging monitors and saw that they were at 20% and climbing. A smile crept across his face, and his tears turned into tears of joy.

CHAPTER 13:
DELEANAA

James looked around the Great Hall. The members of the court, the finely dressed guests, and all in attendance were silent. He could hear the crystal sequins adorning the ladies' gowns chime melodically whenever one of them shifted in place. His mouth felt dry as he became acutely aware of everyone's attention on him. He'd never been fearful of public speaking, but at this moment, he wished he could disappear into a discreet corner.

After what seemed like an uncomfortably long silence, the King stepped forward, clasping James' shoulders with both hands. "Rejoice!" he told him. "You have emerged from your dark journey into the light, and the gods look favorably upon you. Tonight we celebrate! And tomorrow we will assist your return home."

Applause filled the hall as the Queen stepped forward to stand by the King's side. "Tonight you are our honored guest!" she said. "Feast with us. Enjoy the entertainment and be merry. Tomorrow at sunrise, we will set you on your path home."

The King waved over his secretary, who shuffled over to James and bowed deeply. "See to it that our guest is outfitted with a ship and all that he will need to return to Earth," the King instructed his somber assistant. "Send also samples of our best crystals as a parting gift."

The King's warm gaze fell again upon James. "We hope you'll return in friendship so that we can properly discuss a long-term trade arrangement. We've long wished to form an alliance with Earth and to learn more about your biological design technologies."

"Thank you! That would be a great honor," James said, bowing deeply to both sovereigns. He felt a wave of relief and gratitude for the King's generosity. Tomorrow would begin a new chapter: his long-awaited homecoming.

The King and Queen returned to their thrones; the music started up again. James took his seat at a side table, and food and drink were placed in front of him.

Deleanaa came over and sat beside him, her long, slender arms nearly touching his tunic. Her smooth skin appeared to be almost translucent in contrast to the dark folds of her gown, and she carried with her the scent of a delicate and eerily beautiful alien flower.

A tingling electric shock passed through James when Deleanaa's hand momentarily brushed against his arm. "You've come even farther than I had imagined," Deleanaa said in her musical voice.

"What had you imagined, Deleanaa, princess of Ectara?" James replied politely.

She smiled at him. "Please, call me Anaa. That is what my friends call me—no need for formalities." She placed her hand on his.

James altogether forgot his age and felt as though he were a schoolboy once again. "I will see to it that some presents are placed on your ship to bring home to your family," she said warmly.

Deleanaa was kind to extend her generosity to include his family, and her altruism only made him admire her more. "You are too kind, Anaa," he said. "I can see that your beauty is a reflection of your inner goodness. The King and Queen are very lucky to have you as a daughter."

Deleanaa searched James' face. While she found James to be a curiosity and an attractive and well-spoken man, she knew she was destined to marry a noble Ectaran diplomat and continue in her parent's footsteps. "James, I can tell you are a good man with a kind heart. I too wish for you every happiness possible, and for your family as well," she said, then slowly stood and walked away. His eyes followed her graceful figure as she moved through the room.

The sun was just peeking above the calm blue ocean when the King's men put the last of the supplies onboard the ship that had been outfitted for James. The swift vessel sat on a narrow landing dock that steeply rose 500 meters out of the ocean. Waves crashed on the rocks below.

James and Deleanaa walked across the narrow crystal bridge to the ship. When they reached it, James looked at her, preparing to say farewell.

Without saying anything, she pinned a crystal pendant onto a fold of his tunic. He bowed deeply and took his leave of the lovely princess as the King and Queen watched from the other side of the bridge.

James felt bittersweet about departing this beautiful land and its kind people. He was thrilled beyond belief to finally be back on a path home, but at the same time, he was sad to be leaving such a welcoming place. Behind the royal family, the crystal palace glittered in the morning light.

James sat down at the helm, and the sleek vessel lifted him straight up into the air. It hovered for a few moments before disappearing in a flash of light. "Set a course for Earth, maximum warp," James said.

"Setting course for Earth," the computer responded. "Maximum warp. Estimated travel time is 12 hours and 23 minutes."

The stars hung around him, bright points in the black void of space, then elongated into streams of light as the ship jumped into warp.

CHAPTER 14:

IN DARKNESS

The office was dark—all of the glow plants had been turned off. Ella was dressed entirely in black. She nimbly and silently made her way through the office, crawling under desks and crouching behind cabinets, moving carefully so as not to be detected by the sensors. She knew where all the cameras were placed and which spots to avoid.

Ella hated breaking into her own office. It made her feel cheap and childish, like a troubled teenager shoplifting from the community store down the street. Still, she knew she needed a little more time to figure out her next plan. She just couldn't let the company be taken over by the board of directors! James might still be out there— she couldn't give up yet. If those corporate pirates had their way, they'd abandon all attempts to search for him and let him waste away in the vastness of space. She needed to maintain some semblance of control over the company, not only to keep his seat warm for his return, but also to have access to the company's resources so that she could continue to search for James.

Ella let herself into Project Loom's office and set to work hacking into the computer. She located the weekly progress and started uploading the data to an anonymous offshore server. Just as she was ready to press "delete," she heard a familiar and unwelcome voice say "Lights on."

As the glow plants brightened up the room, Vince stepped out from behind a doorway. "Really, Ella? How long did you think you could get away with this?" he asked her harshly.

Ella remained silent. She hated the sight of his tall, athletic figure and wavy blonde hair speckled with gray. There was something unmistakably evil in the arch of his eyebrows.

"Did you really think no one would notice?" Vince continued as he stepped closer to her.

Ella didn't answer. She forced herself to her feet and then stood still, pinned to the spot. Frustration, anger, and fear overwhelmed her. She felt frozen, like a deer in headlights.

"Should anyone else find out about this, you'll lose everything!" Vince told her angrily. "The company, your reputation, everything you and James worked for all those years. Gone in an instant!"

He paced in a circle and stopped right behind her, placing his hands on her shoulders. She shuddered at his touch. "But I'm not like those judgmental people," he said in a softer tone. "I can see that your motives are for the right reasons. James was a lucky fellow to score a bird like you. He'd be proud of how you've championed him." His voice dropped into a near-whisper. "But Ella, I was his friend, and I can tell you that he wouldn't want you to wait for him forever."

He came around to face her. "Let's put this behind us. There's no reason anyone needs to know what you've been doing." His voice grew louder and harder. "Or at least, *I* certainly won't mention it if you do the smart thing. Tomorrow night, at the annual shareholder's gala, make your recommendation for the next CEO: me."

He leaned in closer, bringing his face against her cheek as he whispered, "This can be our little secret. The first of many, I hope." He reached up and ran one hand over her breasts, sliding the other down towards her groin.

She spun around and tried to slap him across the face, but he caught her hand and twisted it behind her back. He forced his mouth on hers and started ripping her shirt down the center. She struggled to get away, but Vince was taller and stronger. He pinned her down on the floor, ripping off her pants.

"Noooo!!! Stop it! Get off me!!" she screamed. But it was too late—he was already inside her. At some point, she stopped struggling and let him have his way. Maybe if she stopped fighting, he'd finish faster. A minute later, when he was finally done, he got up and wiped himself off on a scrap of her shirt that had fallen to the ground.

As he walked away, he said dismissively, "Delete any footage of this little encounter. I'm sure you wouldn't want your son Max to know what a tart his mother really is."

Ella felt cold and distant. She was not even sure she was in her own body.

He turned and paused. "After the gala, we can celebrate our new working relationship in my room," he said, smirking.

Ella was still on the floor, unable to move and unable to process what Vince was saying. After he was halfway down the hallway, she looked down and realized he'd left a hotel key card in her hand.

She went home in a daze. She took a long shower, trying to wash away his scent and fluids. Afterwards, she sat on the floor of the bathroom for a long time. Hot tears streamed down her cheeks uncontrollably. Although Ella was almost 50, she felt like a little girl—helpless, hurt, and unable to take control of her feelings. She crawled into bed and allowed sleep and the forgetfulness of dreams to soothe her aching soul.

The next morning, Ella woke up feeling slightly better. Part of her wanted to believe the previous day had just been a terrible dream. She almost felt like she could trick herself into believing it hadn't happened at all. Perhaps believing that would help her get on with the day, she decided.

She went into the kitchen and fumbled with the coffeemaker. Normally, Hestia made coffee for her, but after what had happened, Ella just wanted to do one thing by herself. She took apart the filter and rinsed it in the sink. As water ran over her hands, she felt tears streaming down her cheeks again. Where were all those tears coming from? How did she even have enough fluid in her body for the constant stream of warm, salty tears?

She wiped them away and tried to reassemble the coffeemaker, but with her blurry vision, she couldn't quite get the filter to fit back into place. Frustrated, she threw the entire coffeemaker across the room. It hit the wall with a thud, and brown water splattered onto the floor. Just another thing to add to her list of failed attempts.

Max had only gotten home from the Asian Union a few hours ago and had fallen asleep in the living room. He woke at the loud crashing sound. "Mom?" he said, entering the kitchen and rubbing his eyes.

She looked at him, tears still sliding down her cheeks. "He's coming home. You were right—we just have to wait."

Max ran to her and grabbed her hands, squeezing them with excitement.

"How was the trip?" she asked him before he could mention her tears. She tried to hold them back and smile at her son.

Max could barely contain himself. "It was great—Michael had a transmission from Dad. He's alive! He's on his way here. He's coming home!"

Ella was silent for a long time; her cheeks and nose turned a deeper shade of red. "Coming home?" she finally repeated.

"Yes, Mom, Dad's coming home!" Max said, still grinning. He finally let go of her hands, and she hastily turned and picked up a dishtowel, using it to blot her face.

"When?" was all she could say.

Max's expression turned slightly somber as he looked at his mother. "I don't know. But I know we just have to hang in a little longer," he said reassuringly. He expected his mother to look comforted, but instead tears started pouring down her face again.

"What if we can't wait any longer?" Ella sobbed.

"What are you talking about?" Max asked, looking alarmed.

Ella sniffled. "That creep Vince caught me. He knows what I've been up to, and he's threatened to expose me unless I propose that he be the next CEO at tonight's gala."

Max frowned and started tidying the kitchen, picking up the coffeemaker and filter and toweling the spilled coffee off of the floor. "You can't do that!" he said as he was reassembling the coffeemaker.

"I know," Ella agreed. "We have to buy some time."

Max looked around the now-clean room. "I think I have an idea," he said excitedly.

Ella watched his eyes light up with a new scheme and started to feel slightly hopeful herself.

CHAPTER 15

HOMECOMING

The island was surrounded by a cloud of mist. James landed his ship on the beach near his old office, glad that the thick, heavy fog hid his ship from view.

He stepped out of the ship and fell to his knees on the sand. For twenty years he'd dreamed about this moment of returning home. So many times over the past two decades, he had thought he would never make it, would never step foot again upon his familiar island, the place where he felt he belonged. But now, at long last, he had returned!

Grasping fistfuls of sand, he watched it fall through his fingertips before he bent down to kiss the earth. Some sand got in his mouth, and he spat out the gritty grains. He was so happy to be back he didn't even mind the earthy taste they left in his mouth. He wiped his face on his sleeve, stood up slowly, and walked up the steep hill, heading inland.

Every breath of fresh air was sweeter than the last. James could scarcely believe he was seeing the island where he had grown up. *I'm home! I'm home!* he kept thinking. It felt so good to be back. He recognized every tree, and every rock felt familiar; there was something about the island that just felt "right" in his bones.

James kept walking towards the office. He looked very different now than when he had left for Hectar—he was not sure if anyone would even recognize him. Deep-set lines creased his brow, and his beard and hair were speckled with white. His face was worn from the darkness of war and the troubles he had endured on his journey home. At the same time, he was dressed in finely woven Ectaran clothes.

As he approached the office, he saw smartly dressed professionals walking into the lobby. Their youthful and chipper demeanors made James pause and momentarily examine himself. When had he grown so old? *These employees look like children!* He couldn't help thinking. He took a deep breath and followed one in through the entrance.

James crossed the lobby and headed straight for the stairs that led to the bio-engineering labs on the second floor. The lobby's vaulted ceiling was made of genetically engineered mariposa trees that each spanned 100 meters. The live trees had never ceased to instill a sense of awe in everyone, including James. Even though he had been one of the lead designers in creating this architectural masterpiece, he could scarcely believe its majesty himself.

Looking around, James was stunned to see that everything was exactly as he remembered. Just at that moment, Robert walked down the stairs, idly reading a salacious business news article about how a prominent fund manager had committed suicide after having been caught misappropriating funds. Completely oblivious to anything else, Robert walked right past James, only glancing up momentarily. He continued on his way without pause, not recognizing his own Chief Executive Officer.

James watched from a distance as Robert walked into the multi-purpose room. Robert paused to put away his tablet, and James looked past him to see a flurry of activity going on in the room. It looked like a big event was about to take place: servers were setting up tables, carpenters were assembling an elaborate stage, and a team of workers was rolling out an oversized ice sculpture carved into the shape of a tree with a hundred outstretched branches. Giant cages containing glowing Blue Morpho butterflies simultaneously decorated and illuminated the room.

"No, no, no!" James heard Robert scold the employees. "I said *ten* thousand butterflies, not *one* thousand. This just won't do. More! We need many more!"

James edged closer to the room. He saw a woman who must be the event planner hesitantly approach Robert. "Sir, my apologies," he heard her say. "That just wasn't in the budget for the event."

Robert's face flushed a deep scarlet, and pronounced blood vessels popped up around his nose and cheeks. "Tonight must be spectacular," he snapped. "Charge it to the company and make it happen! I'll see to it that it's approved." He crossed his arms and examined the bar. "And be sure to serve the good stuff. Break out the rare vintages from the company's private collection. Tonight should be a night to remember!" The woman frantically made some notes in her tablet, nodding.

Must be the annual meeting, James thought. *They've really gone nuts this year.* That realization bothered him—why was it going to be such a big affair?—but he decided to keep going in the opposite direction. He had one goal: to find Ella.

James walked up to the second floor, where engineers were busy working at their desks. Ella's office and the conference room were empty, so he kept going, peering into every room. At one point, he thought he saw Ella leaning against an engineer's desk. It looked as though they were discussing something, but her face was obscured by her long, wavy auburn hair.

James felt his heart start to race as walked over to her—he could scarcely believe he was finally about to be reunited with his wife. Then she looked up, and James saw her face. His heart sank when he realized that she was not Ella.

The unfamiliar woman stood up and approached James. "Can I help you?" she asked.

There was an awkward silence as James stared at her hair for a moment too long. It bore an uncanny resemblance to that of his wife. "No," he finally blurted out. "I mean, yes." He attempted to regain his composure. "I'm looking for Ella."

"Oh, you must be here for the annual meeting. She's not in today, but she'll be here tonight. Can I leave a message for her?" the woman asked.

"Thank you, but that won't be necessary," James said, turning to leave.

He exited the office unnoticed and started walking towards the home he and Ella and Max had shared. *I hope I can still find them there,* he thought with a twinge of nervousness.

The mist around the island had created a damp autumnal gloom. Still, despite the overcast skies, James kept passing familiar sights that warmed his heart. Before he had built up his father's company, Ithaca had been little more than a small island village, with more goats than people. It still had all of its original natural charm, and the rocky cliffs, stony beaches, and blue waters registered in his heart as home. This where he was supposed to be.

Wildflowers sprouted up here and there, splashes of color cheering him along his path home. Since the company had become an interstellar conglomerate, the island's population had grown in number, but partly due to the green "living homes" the company grew from genetically designed trees, the island's character had remained mostly unchanged. The architectural relics of the past and the new green designs of the present harmoniously co-existed—old historic buildings sat alongside the new tree houses, and the two styles blended together as though they had always both been there.

The sun was hanging low in the sky by the time James reached home. He walked up the well-worn lane and placed his hand on the door. It recognized his bio-print and opened.

Hestia greeted him in the foyer with a shriek of joy. "Happy to see you back, sir!!" the android said with unusual emotion. Even though James looked quite different now, she had recognized him immediately.

"Happy to be back, old pal!" James replied. Hestia took his cloak and hung it in the closet. "Where are Ella and Max?"

"Ella's just gone out," Hestia replied. "She's headed to the office for the annual gala. Max is in his room."

James' heart skipped a beat at the mention of his son. He still remembered Max as a little boy with round cheeks and plump legs, but of course he was much older now. James was slightly terrified to find out who his little boy had become and what Max would think of his father. James had never thought he would be away so long—the original plan had been three years, or perhaps five. It had never occurred to James that five years would stretch into twenty. He felt guilty for having missed so many critical years in his son's development. *What would it have been like to grow up without a father?* he wondered.

James walked down the hall and paused in front of Max's room. Then, taking a deep breath, he opened the door.

Max was sitting at his desk, working on his tablet.

"Max?" James said, still hardly believing this was really happening.

Max turned around. "Dad???" His eyes went wide with surprise and joy.

Seeing each other for the first time after so many years, they both recognized the uncanny resemblance they bore to one another. Not only did they resemble one another physically, they also noticed something similar about their presence and the way they carried themselves. It seemed like they were mirror images of one another in presence, personality, and character.

Slowly, Max got up and walked to his father. They threw their arms around one another, hugging for the first time since Max was a baby. Tears of joy ran down their cheeks.

CHAPTER 16:

HESTIA

Hestia was overjoyed to see James return. Once again, her family was complete! Her programming had included basic humanoid emotions such as joy and loyalty, and she had greeted James with as much enthusiasm as her android interface would accommodate. Although his physical appearance had changed, she had recognized him immediately by his facial structure and retinal print.

Hestia could immediately tell based on his skin texture that he was aging at an accelerated rate, perhaps due to harsh conditions and stress associated with space travel and war. She covertly scanned his body with her ultrasound detectors and noticed no unusual abnormalities—all organs seemed to be operating at the normal levels associated with his age.

Hestia took pride in charting the health status of her family and making them aware of any alarming abnormalities so they might be addressed as soon as possible. A couple years ago, she had noticed that Ella's hormone levels were slightly elevated. Ella saw her doctor right away. It turned out that she had a slightly overactive thyroid. Thanks to Hestia, Ella had her genetic code analyzed and adjusted and had been in excellent health ever since.

The years had passed steadily for Hestia. There was usually something that needed to be done, and if Ella and Max didn't need anything, she used her creative programing to come up with ways to be useful: learning how to prepare a new dish, reorganizing miscellaneous items around the house, optimizing the programming of the other household devices. It pleased Hestia to think she had been truly helpful these past years, alleviating at least a little of the burden on the family while James was away.

After greeting James and taking away his dirty clothes, Hestia set about finding clean pressed garments and preparing some of his favorite dishes, like rignando with oregano, olive oil, chopped tomatoes, and feta; and savoro, a marinated fish dish that James' mother used to make. She set the table and then headed for James' bedroom.

Although Ella had asked Hestia to put James' clothes into storage some years ago, Hestia had continued to wash and press them quarterly in anticipation of his return. Now, assuming that he would be attending the annual meeting, Hestia had taken the liberty of steaming his formal attire and laying it out on the bed.

As she walked down the hallway, she overheard James and Max. Their voices were muffled, but due to Hestia's sensitive microphone implants, she could clearly hear every word.

"I'm sorry I missed so much of your childhood, son," she heard James say, his voice cracking.

"That doesn't matter, Dad. The important thing is that you're here now," Max replied.

Hestia had overheard many conversations about James' absence over the years. When Max was six, he had thrown an especially severe temper tantrum, crying, "How come Daddy doesn't come back for us? He doesn't love us! If he did, he would be here with us!" Ella had tried to explain the complexity of the situation, but it was mostly lost on six-year-old Max.

Hestia was pleased that now Max was thrilled to have his father back home. Through sobs of joy from the two men, Hestia overheard

Max tell James what had transpired in his absence. She wasn't surprised when she eventually heard James call out her name.

"Hestia," he said, "we're going to need your help!"

CHAPTER 17

THE BOARD OF DIRECTORS

The band had started up and was playing old jazz classics, and amuse-bouche were being passed around on trays. Employees, shareholders, the board of directors, and friends and family were drifting in. They helped themselves to food and drink as they socialized and cheerfully made small talk. A few brave souls danced, but for the most part, the dance floor was empty.

Upstairs, Ella watched the scene from her corner office. She was dressed in a red gown made of living fish scales that had been genetically spliced with jellyfish bioluminescence. The mermaid-like train of the dress sparkled and glowed in the light of the setting sun, and black obsidian earrings dangled against her wavy auburn hair.

Ever since James had left, she had never liked these annual galas. Each year, she had felt a growing pressure to pass the torch, yet she had also felt increasingly determined to dig in and hold out for the return of her husband.

Ella could see that Vince was doing shots at the bar with a few well-dressed investors. They were laughing at a joke he had just told, no doubt something crude. Although Vince had just turned 50, Ella thought he still had the humor and demeanor of a schoolboy. She looked at the time and reluctantly decided that she should probably start heading downstairs.

Meanwhile, James and Max entered the party using the service entrance. They tucked themselves into a corner and observed the scene from the shadows. In the midst of the festivities, no one noticed them.

James' heart stopped when he saw Ella enter. It seemed like the entire room paused for a moment; all eyes fell on Ella. Completely oblivious to the attention she commanded, Ella made her way across the busy floor to Vince.

They kissed on both cheeks. "I trust you've given it some thought?" Vince said, momentarily taken in by her lovely appearance.

"Yes, I have, and I'm ready to make the announcement," Ella said sincerely.

"Excellent! Fantastic. I couldn't be happier. I hope you haven't lost that key I gave you?" Vince smirked. His hand wandered around her back and squeezed her behind.

"No, I haven't." Ella said, forcing a smile. "It's right where I left it." Specifically, it was in her trash dispenser upstairs.

Ella took a drink off a tray as a server passed by. She gave Vince another tight smile and then walked away. She could feel his eyes following her as she moved through the crowd. Moments later, the investors were laughing at his antics again. Ella suspected the amusement was at her expense.

The room started to fill up, and Ella took a seat at a table in front. A server brought her a plate of radicchio and endive salad with black truffles and roasted walnuts. She noticed a note tucked under her plate. It read "Meet me in the back, behind the speakers. J."

What?? Is that James?? He must be back! she thought, frantically trying to keep her face expressionless. *And he doesn't want everybody to know it...* She took a bite as calmly as possible, then excused herself and made her way towards the speakers, passing the occasional dancer. She walked behind the speakers, her eyes darting everywhere. When a hand touched her on the shoulder, she whirled around.

For the first time in years, Ella and James looked at one another. A curious fluttering feeling suddenly overwhelmed James; he felt nervous and giddy at the same time. "You're even more beautiful now than the day I first met you," James said softly, overtaken with emotion.

Ella's gaze swept up and down his figure—she could barely believe her eyes. She searched his face to make sure he was really her husband. Even though he had showered and shaved and was wearing one of his own custom tuxes, after twenty years of war and space travel, James had aged substantially, and for a second, Ella was worried that this might be an imposter trying to trick her.

Then she saw the mischievous sparkle in his blue eyes and the soft smile lines that had marked his face even all those years ago at university. Her fears vanished, and a warmth of joy washed over her heart.

"You don't look so bad yourself," Ella joked. She stepped in closer, taking his hand.

Just then, the music stopped and the MC made an announcement. "I give you interim CEO Ella Odysseus!" his voice boomed out.

Ella exchanged a knowing look with James and squeezed his hand before letting go and walking to the stage. She stood before the microphone and looked out at the many people who had gathered for the event.

"Friends," she said, addressing the room. "We gather here tonight to celebrate another successful year. I am pleased to announce that Project Loom is finally complete!"

Cheers all around made her pause. "I know it took a little longer than we had expected," she continued once the applause started to die down. "But let me tell you, it was worth the wait! Project Loom is poised to deliver smart clothing to protect and treat soldiers, first responders, and other at-risk individuals who place their lives on the line to help the rest of us."

She paused again, this time for effect. "I can tell that some of you are wondering what the outcome of all of our research will be— Robert, I see you looking puzzled over there."

He gave her a slight grin as a few people laughed. "Let me put your fears to rest: Project Loom will also be very profitable for our bottom line." The room laughed again and applauded.

Now to the main attraction, she thought, and took a deep breath. "As promised, I am prepared to make my recommendation for a permanent CEO." Her gaze swept the crowd; she saw Vince smirking to himself as he straightened out his shirt. He was obviously ready to jump up onto the stage and accept her recommendation.

"It is with great pleasure that I introduce a man who needs no introduction: James Odysseus!" Ella announced.

James stepped out of the shadows and walked onto the stage. The room went quiet. Vince had just taken a sip of his champagne, and everyone heard him choke and spit it onto the floor.

James took the microphone, smiling at his wife. "It's good to be back. Ella, you've done an amazing job as CEO in my absence!"

Ella nodded, matching his smile with one of her own. James turned to face the audience. "I'd like to thank Ella for her hard work, and I'd also like to thank the board of directors for providing guidance and sage counsel. And of course, I'd like to thank our investors, business partners, and employees—you are the backbone of this company. You *are* this company."

Wild cheers erupted into the silence; everyone except Vince was clapping and shouting their approval. "As I've been away for a while," James said into the hubbub, "I'd like to ask the board to meet with me in the conference room right now." He grinned at everyone. "Thank you for coming! Please enjoy yourselves," he said, then stepped off the stage. The band started up again.

A long table sat in the middle of the conference room. Max was already sitting there when James and Ella and the board members sifted into the room.

James took the seat at the head of the table. "I understand that a number of you had expressed an interest in taking on additional leadership roles in my absence," he began.

Robert interrupted him. "You're gone for twenty years and then you show up out of the blue…and now it's back to business as usual? This is highly irregular!"

"Robert," Vince cut in, "where are your manners? Here is our hero who has returned from space travel and war and who knows what else. James, old sport, good to have you back!" He gave him an insincere smile.

"Good to be back," James said, eying Vince with subdued hostility. Ella shifted uncomfortably in her chair.

Vince's smile turned into a carefully modulated frown. "But although I dislike Robert's approach, there is some truth to his words. How do we know you are prepared to take on corporate responsibilities when you've been gone so long? Have you had a medical evaluation? Many returning from war suffer from debilitating PTSD. I can't even imagine what you've endured these past twenty years…" Vince let his voice trail off suggestively.

James felt his ears start to burn and his cheeks turn red. He paused before speaking to rein in his mounting anger. "That is a reasonable question," he said evenly. "Perhaps I might have the same concerns if the tables were turned. However, I am ready to resume my duties as CEO. Remember, I took over this company when I was not much older than my son Max is now." He glanced at Max as he spoke; Max gave him a proud grin.

"My father founded this company, but I built it up—there is no one more qualified to run it," James said firmly. "I've had more than enough time to think things through, and I've seen and learned things across the galaxy that will serve us well." He pulled a small box out of his pocket and placed it gently on the table.

Everyone leaned in curiously as James opened the box. "This is sustainable crystal tech," he explained. "It's a gift from the Ectarans. We can incorporate these new chemical compounds into numerous new projects for years to come. I've also established favorable relations with their government, and they've invited us to return and begin a trade alliance."

"That's all well and good," Vince said dismissively. "And if it were up to me, I wouldn't stand in your way. But this is a public company, not a private business, and as such, the board of directors has a fiduciary duty to our investors to direct and oversee what is best for the company. The board is behind me now, old sport. Quite simply, I have the votes."

Vince looked around the room triumphantly. "I move to remove James as CEO," he announced.

"Seconded," said Robert.

Vince could no longer repress his grin. "All in favor?" he asked.

All of the board members except for James and Ella raised their hands.

"Wait!" James said, holding up a hand. "Before we record that vote, I think there is something you need to see."

He gestured to Max. His son tapped his tablet, turning on the holographic projector in the center of the table. Images came into focus and floated above the table.

"Contrary to what I said publicly back there and public perception, you've taken advantage of your positions to the detriment of this company. Had it not been for Ella's steadfast stewardship, I have no doubt you would have run it into the ground," James said bluntly. "You've been throwing excessive parties, running up your expense accounts, and brokering sweetheart deals that ultimately didn't pan out."

As he spoke, images of parties, headlines, and documents appeared. "On top of that, we've found the following details that I think you'd prefer were *not* made public."

He and Max exchanged glances, and then Max got up and walked around the table, handing a tablet to each board member. They turned them on and glanced over the material briefly. Some turned red; one raised an eyebrow. Robert looked like he was sick to his stomach. Vince was the only one who remained calm.

One by one, they all turned their tablets off—they had seen enough of their personal indiscretions to know that they should comply with James and hope that the current embarrassing ordeal disappeared quickly and quietly.

"Of course, no one has to know about any of this." James looked hard at Vince and then met each of the board members' eyes in turn.

Ella seized the opportunity. "I move to strike the previous motion from the record and reinstate James as the CEO. The *permanent* CEO."

"Seconded," Robert said quickly.

Ella looked triumphant. "All in favor?"

All hands went up around the room. Even Vince reluctantly raised his hand when he saw that he had lost.

"Motion approved!" Ella said. She didn't try to hide the happiness in her voice.

James gave them all a satisfied smile. "Very well! I'll see that these are safely tucked away," he said as Max collected the tablets and handed them to James. "Oh, and one other thing," he added as everyone stood.

They looked at him uncertainly. "I'll accept your resignation letters in the morning," James said calmly. He could tell by their expressions that his statement wasn't exactly a surprise. He smiled at them again and nodded. "Meeting adjourned."

The board filed out of the room. As soon as the last one had left, James and Ella embraced for the first time since he had left for Hectar.

Max shook his head and looked away, embarrassed by their display of affection. Still, though, he was overjoyed to see his parents reunited. "Get a room already," he muttered. He was only half joking.

CHAPTER 18

IN THE BEDROOM

Back at home, James showered and washed off the dirt and grime of the day. The meeting with the board had gone as well as could be expected, he felt, yet the experience of resorting to blackmail to remove the board members had made him feel cheap. But it had been a brilliant plan…and Max had been the one to think of it. *At 22, Max is not really so "young" anymore*, he thought ruefully. At the same time, he was amused by his son's clever plan. It reminded him of a bit of his own mischievous ingenuity in his younger years.

But despite his triumph, James couldn't stop thinking about Vince and the smug look on his face in the board room. He knew what had happened the day before, and that knowledge made him want to track Vince down and pummel him into oblivion.

Prior to the gala, James had hacked into the company's security feed to look for incriminating surveillance footage to use as leverage. He was sure he would find something illegal or indecent that the members had done, but he never would have thought he'd see Vince attack Ella. Ever since then, he had been imagining ways to exact retribution. The only thing that had stayed his hand was the knowledge that any violent act would only hurt Ella more, and that was the last thing he wanted to do.

He vowed to stop thinking dark thoughts; instead, he took a shower and let thoughts of death and destruction wash down the drain. Refreshed, James toweled off and emerged from the bathroom.

He slid into bed beside Ella. For a few moments, they held hands and looked up at the high ceiling created by branches growing together in a vaulted formation.

"Skylight open," James said. The intertwined aspen branches opened, revealing the stars overhead. Ella shifted to rest her head on his shoulder.

"There's something I should probably tell you," James said.

Ella's heart sank. After twenty years apart, she knew many things must have happened to her husband, any number of which probably had the potential to destroy their marriage. Admittedly, she was also curious to hear his stories…but in the last twenty years, she had become wise enough to know that she would rather start afresh and move forward than go down a potentially destructive rabbit hole of truth-seeking.

She raised her head to meet his gaze. "You're here, and that's everything I need to know," she said, placing her hand over his heart. He nodded wordlessly.

Ella told James about the lonely years she had spent trying to keep the business afloat, fighting with the board of directors and sending out search-and-rescue efforts to find him. "I never gave up hope," she said, pausing to hold him a bit tighter. She told James all about Max: what he was like as a boy, how brilliant and funny he was growing up, how he had also never given up on his father returning.

Once she had finished, James pointed to constellations in the sky and recounted bits and pieces of his voyage home. They laughed at the antics of his men when they forgot themselves on Decta, and Ella held James tightly again as he told her about the AI creatures that had destroyed nearly his entire fleet of ships. She wondered at the Owellis and the visions James had experienced in the wormhole, and she wiped his tears as he told her about losing all of his men.

Finally, he paused to kiss her. She snuggled against him even more closely as they watched a few shooting stars dart across the sky. Their soft voices painted stories into the late hours of the night and mingled with the sounds of cicadas, rustling aspen leaves, and the distant rolling tides beyond the shores.

MEET THE CHARACTERS

 **James** was born on Ithaca and educated in England. He met his wife Ella when he was a student at Oxford. He is a storyteller, inventor, husband, and father. Cunning and smart, James uses his intellect and intuition to solve problems and overcome insurmountable odds. James is stoic, charming, deeply flawed, and also loveable. He is the founder of Olive, a successful plant engineering and architectural company. Olive invested in Project Stella, prompting James to reluctantly lead a rescue mission to retrieve Stella from Hectar.

 **Ella** grew up in Woodside, California. Her father was a professor at Stanford University and her mother was a psychologist. Ella was a Rhodes scholar at Oxford when she met James. They married a few years after graduating and soon had a son, Max. Ella is James' other half, steadfast and intelligent. When James is away at war, Ella takes over the family business, Olive, which designs plant-based houses, vehicles, lighting, etc. The company has been highly successful over the years, expanding into technology and space travel through a series of strategic acquisitions. When James leaves to retrieve Stella, Ella keeps the company afloat and does her best to prevent the board of directors from running the company into the ground.

Max is James and Ella's son. Max was barely two years old when James left. Although Max couldn't remember his father, as he grew up, he studied pictures, videos, and social media to try to understand who his father was. Max travels to the Asian Union on his mother's behalf to meet with his father's friend, Michael.

Michael is James' friend and the lead designer of Stella. He lives in a part of the Asian Union that in the present day would be China. Michael's tech design company also sends a rescue mission to Hectar, but they are unsuccessful. James uses their inter-Stellaes communications system, "Hermes," to send Michael a message from thousands of light years away, asking Michael to tell his family that he is still alive and on his way home.

Hestia is Ella and James' household android; she is an intelligent and helpful artificial life form. Hestia helps with housework, childcare, cooking, and other miscellaneous tasks at home.

The board of directors of Olive performed their duties adequately while James was CEO, but after ten years of war and then another ten years of James being absent, their leadership goes amuck—decadent parties have replaced quarterly meetings, and sweetheart deals have started eating into the company's bottom line.

Vince is one of James' oldest friends—they went to boarding school together and were friends at Oxford. Vince was appointed to the board not long after James took over the family business from his father. After James leaves, Vince tries to capitalize on the opportunity and take control of the company. Vince is an arrogant and narcissistic man who believes he can take whatever he wants and that rules don't apply to him.

Robert is the longest-serving member of the board, but he winds up in Vince's pocket after James leaves for Hectar. Robert and Vince scheme to take over the company, break it up, and sell its parts. Robert is chiefly concerned with lining his own pockets and has very little empathy for others.

The Hectarans are a humanoid race similar to humans. They lived on a vibrant planet, Hectar, which was a trading hub for traveling humanoids. The Hectarans did not embrace clean/green technologies when other planets did, however, and they eventually destroyed their planet with their high carbon footprint, rendering it uninhabitable. Some Hectarans escaped to an enormous spherical spaceship they called New Hectar.

The Stellaes a dozen planets and corporations including James' company Olive, Michael's company from the Asian Union, and Andrew's company from the American Union, are part of an organization of planets that banded together to build "Stella," the most beautiful technology ever created. This united group of beings call themselves the Stellaes. The Stellaes develop a technology that uses the combined gravitational pull of two massive black holes to harvest matter from their singularity to create new planets. Each member of the organization has signed a treaty to defend and protect the technology against any other party that might try to steal or corrupt it for their own purposes. Hoping to rebuild their home planet, the Hectarans steal Stella. Through this action, all other Stellaes are contractually called to war to defend the technology and retrieve Stella.

The Ectarans are a peaceful merchant humanoid race on a remote blue-green planet. They are very technologically advanced.

Deleanaa is a kind and good-hearted Ectaran princess. The only child of the King and Queen, Deleanaa is the heir to the throne of a noble race. She helps James when he is stranded on her planet.

Atara is the leader of an alien and feline-looking band of female pirates who pretend to be stranded on a junk/recycling ship. They entice unwitting crews onboard their ship with their damsel-in-distress act.

First Officer Stewart is a British European Union citizen and James' right-hand man. While James leads from his gut, Stewart is logical and pragmatic.

 **Second Officer Drew** is an African-European Union citizen who was raised in France. He is second-in-command on James' ship. Drew is a natural leader and is well-liked.

 **Science Officer Rajeev** is an Indian-European Union citizen who was raised in England. He was the youngest in his class to graduate from Cambridge, and he went on to get two PhDs: one in astrophysics and one in biochemistry.

 **Communications Officer Francis** is a Chinese-European Union citizen and was raised on Corsica. He grew up speaking the standard English and Mandarin languages of the European, American, and Asian Unions. Later on, he also learned a dozen subdialects and alien tongues, including Hindi, Arabic, Hectaran, Ectaran, Spanish, French, and Swahili.

 **Engineering Officer Thomas** is a Danish-European Union citizen who was raised in Denmark. When other kids were outside playing football, Thomas was taking apart appliances and androids and creating new gadgets. Thomas attended a trade school in Germany before being recruited by a spaceship-manufacturing company.

 **Navigation Officer Eli** is a Jewish-European Union citizen. Eli learned to fly eagle vehicles as a teenager, and by the time he was an adult, he could fly just about anything. Eli also knows star charts inside and out—you could drop him anywhere in the known galaxy and he'd be able to find his way back to Earth blindfolded.

 **Cadet José** is a Latin-European Union citizen. José got high marks in school. He excels at problem-solving and follows direction well.

 **Cadet Jin** is a dual Korean-European Union citizen and Korean-Asian Union citizen. He became the first person in his family to leave his rural village in the Asian Union when he received a scholarship to study in the EU. Eventually, he applied for citizenship there as well. Jin has always dreamed of traveling among the stars.

 **Cadet Rumi** is an Arab-European Union citizen. Raised in Turkey, Rumi also always dreamed of traveling the galaxy. Rumi's father was a cadet, too, but he died on an away mission when Rumi was young. Rumi loves to travel and try new foods.

Pallas is an advanced AI interface for most Earth computers. It is widely adopted in most homes, eagle vehicles, offices and spacecrafts as the go-to computing assistant for a host of activities.

Pod is a small spacecraft for emergency purposes that has limited warp capabilities.

Universal Translator is a software built into most devices such as tablets, computers, spacecrafts and wearables that instantly translates languages and transposes them into brainwaves.

MAP

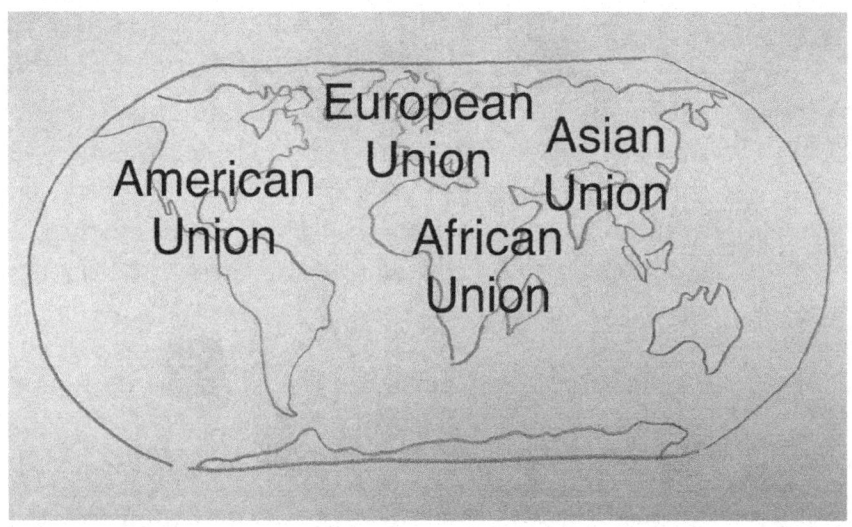

SHIPS

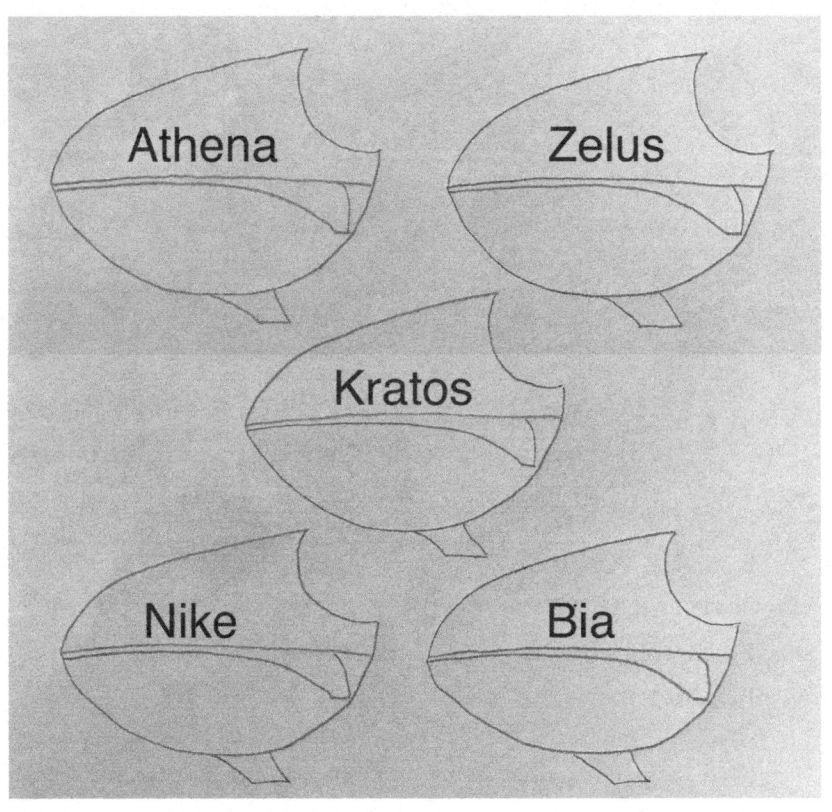

ECTARAN DICTIONARY

In Ectaran, to make most nouns plural, add an -i.
Sometimes possession is shown by adding an -n.

A – Ti

Alas – Wapar

All – Ectareen

And – Ook

As – Qua

At – Gar

Banded – Egara

Battle -- Shatee

Beautiful – Lenaa

Best – Niimba

Biological – Eganatipa

Blood – Linaar

Brightest – Shikala

By – Ieen

Children – Shawali

Clever – Skiisa

Come – Elong

Concealed – Nookala

Corridors – Stopari

Created – Ekongarii

Crossed – Mar

Cunning – Shala

Dark – Krapeet

Demise – Pentii

Despite – Lafar

Devised – Wahaala

Engineer – Sheltatii

Ever – Fara

Fell apart – Kintook

Fiercest – Scala

For – Puk

Fought – Ooteca

Horse – Charrum

Immense – Vegaatar

Impenetrable – Sleetala

In – Elar

Inside – Elarpwi

Into – Elara

It – Sna

Left – Par

Lunatic – Fikasi

Man – Dost

Me – Key

Men – Dosti

Monstrous – Hecataa

Muses – Fotar

Most – Sna

New – Pri

None – Jarg

Not – Sarp

O – Yi

Of – Wa

Offering – Wastaar

Onboard – Lamba

Once – Fleek

One – Yine

Packed – Chariar

Parting – Foogari

Perished – Toomar

Presented – Rastii

Ran – Pepii

Red – Pershi

Retrieve – Wetara

Seam – Foant

Seeming – Egakoom

Space Krapoota

Spaceship – Delonashtar

Spared – Geenar

Spoils – Ringata

Star – Delong

Success – Wishtar

Take – Kant

Take in – Garfelar

Technology – Squeeskar

Ten – Nan

That – Leeka

The – Ha

Their – Asqua

There – Kala

They – Arg

Those – Awelt

To – La

Together – Sherarie

Took -- Garf

Tree – Egamar

Until – Snagar

Victory – Pleaka

War -- Fakar

Warning – Pleekina

Was – Isht

With – Char

Wine – Blita

Whisper – Shetar

Who – Tarp

Woman – Dostari

Would be – Beentar

Years – Deloti

Pronouns:

I – A	We – Arg
You – Ai	You (pl.) Aig
He/She – Ar	They – Arg

Me – Key	Us – Keen
You – Ais	You (pl.) – Aigs
Him/Her – Ary	Them – Aryeen

My – Keaa	Our – Keenaa
Your – Aiaa	Yours – Aigs
Its – Bit	Their – Biti

Verbs:

In Ectaran, verbs go at the end of the sentence. To make a verb in the past tense, you usually add an –ar or –i.

To Be:

I am – A elta	We are – Ag eltar
You are – Ai elate	You (pl.) are – Aig eltaes
He is/She is – Ar Elt	They are – Arg elti

Past Tense To Be:

I was – Ishta	We were – Ishtar
You were – Ishtae	You (pl.) were – Ishtaes
He is/She was – Isht	They were – Ishti

Elizabeth Chang is a writer, director and actress. She received her BA in Interdisciplinary Studies, focusing on Comparative Literature, Classics and Art with Honors from UC Berkeley. She wrote, starred-in, and directed, the tv comedy *The Next Unicorn*, and lives in Los Angeles with her husband and three children.